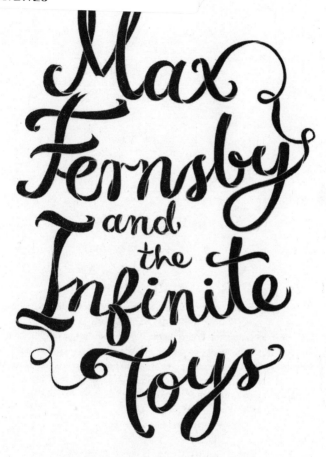

Max Fernsby and the Infinite Toys

GERRY SWALLOW AND **PETER GAULKE**

ILLUSTRATIONS BY **MARTA KISSI**

HARPER

An Imprint of HarperCollinsPublishers

Library of Congress Control Number: 2023933923
ISBN 978-0-06-321475-0

Typography by Torborg Davern
23 24 25 26 27 LBC 5 4 3 2 1

First Edition

For Tom, Liz, Dan, Theresa, and Amy,
the finest siblings one could have
—G. S.

For Hudson
—P. G.

CHAPTER 1

PANTS ON A MOOSE

By now, you probably think you've heard just about every Christmas story ever told. Even if you haven't heard them all, you may feel as though you have, because, let's face it, they're all pretty much the same. They start off with something or someone threatening to stop Christmas. (As if.) Usually it's a cranky green dude (the Grinch), or a terrible blizzard (Rudolph), or a very bad case of constipation (*How the Prunes Saved Christmas*). In the end, everything works out thanks to a change of heart, or a glowing red nose, or a new high-fiber diet.

I can't promise that this story will be all that different, but I can guarantee that you have not heard it before. It is a story of which only I know all the details—and I am telling it now for the very first time.

It all began not too many years ago, with Christmas fast approaching and the North Pole buzzing with excitement and a sense of urgency. Mrs. Claus was stewing prunes by the vatful, while the elves were cranking out toys as fast as they could. Well, most of them were.

Two of these elves were busy with other matters they'd deemed more important. Best friends since their days at North Pole Elementary, Eldor and Skhiff were now in their early two hundreds, which is considered still very young by elf standards. Skhiff was short and scrawny, while Eldor was chubby and tall. Well, tall for an elf. He stood nearly three foot eleven from the soles of his curly shoes to the tips of his pointy ears. Or, more precisely, to the top of his pointy ear, because one of them had been so badly mangled that it now more closely resembled a wadded-up piece of paper. The good news was his damaged ear looked not entirely out of place given the countless injuries Eldor had sustained as a result of the many pranks, stunts, and antics he'd orchestrated—including his latest act of genius, which involved a full-grown moose and a pair of bright plaid pants.

"Run!" Eldor yelled as effectively as one can while giggling hysterically.

"I . . . am . . . running." Skhiff puffed as he struggled to keep up with Eldor, while also struggling to stay ahead of the enormous moose right behind them. The moose was gaining quickly, despite the fact that it had a pair of red-and-yellow plaid pants pulled up over its hind legs.

Eldor glanced over his shoulder and saw that the moose's antlers were mere inches from his best friend's butt. He managed to stop laughing just long enough to yell, "Upshoot!"

The two elves inhaled quickly, filling their lungs with oxygen before shooting up into the air a good twelve feet, high enough to allow the very confused, yet stylishly dressed, moose to run right under them.

(Upshooting, you should know, is really the only magical power that elves have, though actually it's not so much magic as it is simple science. Unlike humans, who breathe in oxygen and convert it to carbon dioxide, elves turn the oxygen to helium, which is why their voices are so high and why they are such good dancers. (They're very light on their feet.) It's also how they manage to get up and down all those chimneys to assist Santa with his Christmas toy deliveries.)

The problem with upshooting is that you can't hold your breath forever, which, in this particular situation, made for a very temporary solution to a very permanent moose.

When Eldor and Skhiff returned to the ground, the highly agitated beast stopped running and whirled around to face the now-breathless elves. Like a snowplow about to clear a city street, the moose lowered its antlers to elf level, groaned audibly, and rumbled forward. Eldor and Skhiff, seeing little other option, desperately ran toward the village, still a good seventy-five yards away.

As they crested the hill and the twinkling lights of the village came into full view, Eldor was the first to notice the thin ribbons of smoke spiraling up from the chimney of the convention center.

"What?" He gasped, momentarily forgetting about his four-legged pursuer. "Are they having a meeting without us? Again?"

Before Skhiff could respond, the moose reminded the elves of his presence by slamming its antlers into their collective backsides with enough force to send them airborne.

"Aaah!" screamed Skhiff, who, unlike his friend, had very little experience when it came to broken bones.

"Upshoot!" yelled Eldor. And when the two elves sucked in all the oxygen they could and held it in, they became like two fast-moving, elf-shaped helium balloons, soaring directly toward the convention center.

Inside the building, the meeting, to which Eldor and Skhiff had intentionally not been invited, had just come to order. Gnurk, Chief Foreman of North Operations and honored member of the International Coalition of Elves, was about to give his annual speech on the importance of teamwork during the last two weeks before Christmas.

Standing at the podium, the middle-aged elf adjusted his reading glasses, then cleared his throat for way too long. (Unless you're a big fan of loose phlegm, it was pretty gross.)

Thankfully, for all in attendance, the sound of mucus

rising up the back of one's throat ended abruptly when Eldor and Skhiff came crashing through the window and tumbled across the meeting hall.

"Eldor? Skhiff? What are you doing here?" asked Gnurk with a frown as the two new arrivals picked themselves off the glass-strewn floor.

"What are we doing here?" Eldor sneered, brushing a few bits of glass from his official forest-green elf suit. "I think the question is, what are we not doing here? Are you having a meeting without us? Again?"

"Unbelievable," said Skhiff, who barely had time to shake his head in disgust before the doors to the hall were blasted open by a full-grown moose in plaid pants. The swinging doors knocked Eldor and Skhiff halfway across the room, where they toppled the refreshment table, sending punch, cookies, cakes, and Joony's famous lemon squares to the floor.

High-pitched, helium-fueled screams filled the air as the moose rumbled through the meeting hall, batting the horrified elves around the room with its antlers.

"This is horrible," shrieked Skhiff from behind the overturned table. "What do we do?"

"Here," said Eldor, plucking a fallen dessert out of the crease of his pants. "When life gives you lemons, eat a lemon square."

"I don't want a lemon square!" shouted Skhiff.

"Suit yourself," said Eldor, taking a big bite as frantic elves rushed for the exit. The stampede created a bottleneck, providing the perfect opportunity for the moose to rush in and scoop up three or four elves at a time and hurl them against the walls and into an upright piano with a rather nonmusical *clang*.

"You know, it's weird to think that someday we'll laugh about this," Eldor mumbled through a mouthful of baked goods.

"How can you say that?" shouted Skhiff over the sounds of tiny bodies landing on things not designed to be landed upon.

Then, just when it seemed the nightmare would never end, in ran two uniformed security elves, each armed with a tranquilizer gun. The first took aim and fired, hitting the moose right in its hind leg. It had no effect, and the moose continued tossing elves around like pointy-eared beanbags. It took a second dart fired into the animal's neck to cause the moose to pass out and for the room to go silent again.

CHAPTER 2

RUNAWAY BEDPAN

At this point in the story, I would like to introduce you to a young man by the name of Max Fernsby. I guess you could say he is the hero of our story, though at first glance he may appear far more reckless than heroic.

"Come on," the ten-year-old daredevil barked out to his friends Baxter and Leoni. "Just push me already!"

Standing on the snow-covered second-story rooftop of an abandoned house, Leoni inched forward to look down at the twenty-foot drop to the front yard below. Though the snow was deep—it was piled nearly as high as the faded For Sale sign planted near the road—Leoni still had some serious doubts.

"I'm sorry, Max, but you're crazy," she said in her raspy voice. "You'll break your foolish neck sledding off this."

"Hey, it's my foolish neck," Max shot back while wiping chunky snowflakes from his eyelashes. "I can break it if I want. Besides, I thought we agreed we would do something Christmasy today. And what could be more Christmasy than riding a toboggan down a snow-covered mountain?"

"Well, first of all," said Baxter, who historically had very little luck talking his friend out of reckless stunts, "this isn't a snow-covered mountain. It's an old abandoned house. And that isn't a toboggan you're sitting on. It's a rusty old bedpan."

For anyone unfamiliar with the item, a bedpan is an oval-shaped metal bowl used as a toilet by people who are unable to get out of bed. They are also occasionally used by poor kids like Max and his friends as a substitute for a proper sled or toboggan.

"Yeah," said Leoni, echoing Baxter's concerns. "And after you break your neck, the bedpan you're riding will come in real handy."

"Fine," said Max at last. "If you won't push me, then I'll do it myself."

Max, who had grown accustomed to having to do things himself since his mother passed away, stood up and plucked the bedpan from the snowy roof. Baxter and Leoni shared a worried look as their friend trudged up to the tip-top of the house. "All I need is a running start."

When he reached the peak, Max turned back toward his worried friends, took a deep breath, and . . . slipped.

Baxter and Leoni watched in horror as Max tumbled, not toward them but down the other side of the house. They scrambled up the roof, reaching the peak just in time to see Max and the bedpan go soaring off the roof toward the ground below. The bedpan hit the ground with a hard *flooph*! Max disappeared in a mushroom cloud of snowflakes before bursting through the side of the snowbank.

Picking up speed as he flew down the sloped backyard, Max headed straight toward a patch of dead weeds. He threw his right forearm across his face for protection as he tore through the tangled cattails and then through a well-placed hole in a chain-link fence. From there he skimmed across the sidewalk, bounced off the curb, and zipped down the icy street that just happened to be one of the steepest in the entire city.

"Oh no, he's heading right down Forty-Third," shrieked Baxter.

"Let's go!" Leoni shouted.

At that very moment on 43rd Avenue, a group of holiday

shoppers looked up to see a young boy sitting on a bedpan rocketing past them down the sidewalk at somewhere in the neighborhood of thirty miles per hour.

Meanwhile, Max was so frightened he was now very close to using the bedpan for its original purpose.

He practically flew down the sidewalk, too fast to appreciate all the signs of Christmas on display: decorations in the storefront windows; colored, flashing lights; festive holly wreaths; the bright-green garlands that spiraled around the lampposts; and a man dressed as Santa Claus, standing in the middle of the sidewalk holding a donation bucket and ringing a bell.

"Look out!" Max screamed as the bedpan blasted the fake Santa's feet out from under him. The collision unfortunately failed to slow Max down one bit, and he plowed into a display of eight plastic reindeer harnessed to a red plastic sleigh. The sled and the reindeer wrapped themselves around Max, and the whole mess bounced along behind him down the street.

Max was too busy trying to untangle himself to notice that down the block, directly ahead of him, a uniformed doorman had just opened the door to a luxury apartment building and out walked a woman dressed in a fur coat with matching fur hat. In her right hand she held four leashes. At the end of each leash was a high-strung dog, yapping and tugging furiously.

"Good morning, Mrs. Miklos," said the doorman with a nod of his head.

"Good morning, Donovan," the fur-clad woman replied just as Max careened into the tangle of leashes that the woman was holding, pulling the yipping and yapping dogs along with him.

"Aaah!" the woman wailed. "Come back, my babies!"

As the dogs ran alongside Max, one of their leashes slid beneath a sidewalk hot dog cart that the vendor had just wheeled into position for the lunchtime crowd. The cart lurched forward and began rolling along with Max, his bedpan, the plastic reindeer, and the four yipping, yapping dogs toward an intersection jam packed with cars, trucks, taxicabs, and one shiny black stretch limousine.

As Max sped toward the intersection, Leoni's prophetic words played in his head. "You'll break your foolish neck." He feared his friend was dead wrong and that he would, instead, break every foolish bone in his body.

CHAPTER 3

THE BOZEMAN INCIDENT

I'm sure you've all seen a stretch limo before, but this one was perhaps stretching things a little too far. Though its interior was not equipped with a Jacuzzi or foosball table, there was more than enough room for such things. And that's because this limo just happened to belong to one of the richest people in the world, the founder and CEO of Rainforest.com.

"I understand they're not happy with the changes to the offer, but whether my competitors are happy with the deal is really none of my concern," scoffed Steve Bozeman into his cell phone as he gnawed on the end of a cigar that cost about the same as a quality used car. "Just so long as the Swinsons sign on the dotted line. And if they refuse to accept this new provision then we'll simply have to back out of the deal and put them out of business. Just like we did with Hinkleman's."

He stuffed his phone into the pocket of his blazer and tugged at the collar of the black turtleneck sweater he always wore to try to hide the fact that he had absolutely no chin whatsoever. "Can't you go a little faster?" he snapped at his chauffeur, inadvertently blowing a thick cloud of cigar smoke into the driver's already-watery eyes.

"Sorry, Mr. Bozeman," the man replied, coughing into his fist. "I can only go as fast as the car in front of me."

"That's just it," said Bozeman, with a quick shake of his head. "We have bike lanes, bus lanes, carpool lanes, and express lanes, but no VIP lanes. What's the use of having money if you can only drive as fast as the loser in front of you?"

Before his driver could answer, Bozeman snapped his fingers and removed his cell phone from his pocket once more. He tapped the screen several times, then spoke into it. "Hover cars. Get patent, mass-produce, sell exclusively on Rainforest. I'll be the world's first trillionaire!"

"That sounds like a very worthwhile goal," said the chauffeur, with no detectable sarcasm.

"Yes," Bozeman agreed. "But at this moment a nonexistent hover car doesn't do me much good. You know what? Just let me out here. I'll walk the rest of the way to the office. It'll be faster, healthier, and probably safer."

For the record, Bozeman was wrong on all counts.

He opened the limo door, stepped onto the sidewalk, and turned to see a terror-stricken boy on a rusty bedpan speeding toward him. The boy was dragging eight plastic reindeer and, not far behind him, were four yappy dogs and a rumbling hot dog cart.

The resulting crash sent Bozeman sprawling, his cigar rocketing from his mouth and into the very large hairdo of a woman walking by. Knocked back into a lamppost, Bozeman slumped to the ground, dazed and bewildered but not to the point that he failed to notice that the hot dog cart had picked up speed and was heading directly toward him.

"Aaah!"

He rolled out of the way just as the cart slammed into the lamppost and tipped over, covering one of the richest men in the world with hot, steaming tubes of meat.

Bozeman exploded in rage when he caught sight of Max, who'd finally come to a stop just a few feet away and was now climbing out from under the tangled mess of plastic reindeer.

"You!" he screamed at the boy. "You . . . you . . . criminal!"

"Sorry, mister," said Max, wiping blood from his lower lip. "It . . . it was an accident."

"An accident? I'll show you an accident, you little street rat."

"Hey, take it easy," said Max, backing away on his hands and knees. "I didn't mean any harm. I'm just a kid."

"You may be a kid, but I will personally see to it that you are tried as an adult and sent to prison for the rest of your life! Come back here!"

Bozeman removed his cell phone from his pocket and aimed it in Max's direction. No sooner had Bozeman snapped the photo than four very excited dogs lunged at him, assuming, by the strong odor of hot dogs, that Bozeman must be made entirely of tube-shaped meat product. And if there was anything Bozeman disliked more than being covered with hot dogs, it was being covered with hot dogs and, at the same time, with regular dogs.

"Get them off me!" he wailed, rolling around on the frozen sidewalk. "Don't you know who I am?"

The yapping schnauzers knew exactly who he was. He was the guy covered in mouthwatering hot dogs. And as they lapped furiously at Bozeman's hot dog–flavored face,

Max stood frozen, watching in astonishment, but only for a second before a gloved hand clamped down upon his shoulder.

"Okay, let's go, buddy."

Looking up, Max was relieved to see that the glove, as well as the hand inside it, belonged to Baxter and not, for instance, the police.

"Come on," Leoni barked. "Let's get out of here while we still can!"

Leoni helped Max to his feet as Baxter gathered up a few loose hot dogs and shoved them into his coat pockets. As his friends began to hustle him away, Max's conscience got the better of him. He turned back to look at the man, screaming in anger and frustration as he wrestled helplessly with the yappy dogs.

"Shouldn't we stay and help him?" Max asked.

"Are you kidding?" said Baxter, continuing to lead Max away from the scene. "A total nobody like you steamrolls a rich dude? What do you think they'll do to you?"

"I guess you're right," said Max, still looking back.

"Of course I'm right," Baxter asserted. "Now let's go."

CHAPTER 4

WE'LL TAKE THE POOP

While it appeared that Max and his friends had emerged from their little adventure unscathed, Eldor and Skhiff were not so lucky. They sat in Gnurk's office enveloped in an uncomfortable silence, interrupted only by the occasional shuffling of paper. Gnurk flipped another page of the huge personnel file, then sighed and shook his head.

With their boss's eyes darting back and forth across the file, Eldor turned in his chair and silently mouthed a message to Skhiff. "I think he's mad."

"What?" Skhiff mouthed back.

Before Eldor could answer, Gnurk yanked his glasses from his face and looked across his desk at the two elves. "I suppose it goes without saying that I am extremely shocked and disappointed," he said. "Your lack of maturity is astounding. It's time you both grew up and stopped acting like a couple of ninety-year-olds. For the life of me I simply cannot understand what would possess someone to try to put pants on a moose."

Eldor raised his right index finger. "Uh, pardon me. Not *try* to put pants on a moose," he corrected. "*Did* put pants on a moose." Eldor turned and offered Skhiff a victory fist bump but was met only with an ice-cold stare.

Gnurk placed his glasses back onto the bridge of his nose and returned his eyes to the file in front of him. "Upon graduation from Elf Academy, you were first assigned to the toy-making division, and you took it upon yourselves to create a battery-powered car that bursts into flames upon impact."

This time it was Skhiff who raised his hand. "I suggested packaging it with a toy fire extinguisher, but that idea was shot down—"

"In flames, you might say," Eldor added with a chuckle. Gnurk's frown quickly wiped the smile from Eldor's face. Skhiff looked away quickly and just in time to catch a glimpse out the window of a snowmobile pulling a flatbed cart. Lying on the cart was a very groggy moose, still very much alive and still very much dressed in a pair of pants that most people, or moose for that matter, wouldn't be caught dead in.

"You were then transferred to the cafeteria," Gnurk continued. "Where you were fired for making an eight-foot-tall *snowman* out of potato salad—"

"Just trying to express ourselves creatively," Skhiff interrupted.

"And leaving it out at room temperature for a week," Gnurk finished.

"You should never put eggs in potato salad," Eldor remarked.

"Yeah, not a fan," said Skhiff, agreeing with Eldor for once.

Normally a quite mild-mannered elf, Gnurk had officially reached his breaking point. "The purpose of this meeting is not to debate the merits of hard-boiled eggs as an ingredient in potato salad," he fumed. "This is about your gross incompetence and lack of professionalism. I will not stand for any more high jinks, shenanigans, or tomfoolery."

Eldor cleared his throat. "What about funny business?"

"No funny business, no horseplay, and no buffoonery!"

"That's a pretty complete list," said Skhiff.

The sudden noise in the room was Gnurk's molars

grinding together. "Listen," he said. "I am way too old to have to deal with this kind of . . ."

"Tomfoolery?" offered Skhiff.

"Yes," said Gnurk. "You two are hopeless. You've even managed to mess up the job of official moose counter, a title we created simply to keep you two out of the way."

"What?" said Eldor, his mouth hanging agape. "Wait a minute. You mean to tell us that moose counting is not a real job?"

"It is not a real job," Gnurk confirmed.

"So we counted all those moose for nothing?"

"Two hundred and eleven moose," said Skhiff, shaking his head.

"Wow," said Eldor. "I don't know quite how to feel right now."

"Betrayed?" Skhiff suggested.

"Betrayed. Yeah, that's it."

Gnurk was not the least bit interested in Eldor's and Skhiff's feelings of betrayal. "You gentlemen have held just about every position available to elves of your skill level, and you've managed to mess up all of them. I'm afraid there's only one job left. Fertilizer relocation engineer."

"Hmm," said Skhiff, pulling at his chin. "Does that involve a lot of travel?"

"It involves a lot of shoveling reindeer manure," said Gnurk flatly.

Looking less than certain, Eldor turned to Skhiff and whispered, "Manure. That's like poop, right?"

"Very similar, yes," Skhiff confirmed.

This was all the additional information Eldor needed. "Yeah, okay. I think we're gonna take a pass on that," he told Gnurk. "Maybe wait for something better to come along."

But Gnurk was having none of it. He slammed his fist down on his desktop with enough force to cause his coffee mug to jump a good couple of inches. "There is nothing better! You're elves. This is it. Your last chance. And if you mess this one up, I'll have no choice but to ship you both off to Greenland."

Eldor scoffed and spat out a fingernail he'd bitten off. "That's it? Greenland? Doesn't sound so bad to me. Nice and green."

"Yeah," Skhiff agreed. "How's the food?"

"In Greenland you are the food," Gnurk replied. "Polar bears."

"Aah, riiight," said Eldor.

"The decision is yours," said Gnurk. "First thing tomorrow morning you can report to the stables and begin shoveling reindeer manure or you can be sent off to

Greenland and end up as bear manure. Shovel or be shoveled. The choice is yours."

Skhiff leaned in close to Eldor to discuss the offer. "I'm thinking shoveling is the way to go," whispered Skhiff, his hand cupped around his mouth.

"Agreed," Eldor whispered back. "Lesser of two evils."

They turned once again to face Gnurk, and Eldor spoke for them both. "Okay," he said. "We'll take the poop."

CHAPTER 5

ONE BIG HAPPY FAMILY

When the bell announcing the arrival of Steve Bozeman's private elevator to the sixth floor of Rainforest headquarters sounded, hearts skipped a beat, palms began to sweat, and eyelids twitched involuntarily. The idle conversation among Rainforest's terrified employees stopped instantly, and everyone rushed around, pretending to work harder than they actually were.

The doors to the elevator slid open with a hiss, and the owner of Rainforest stepped out with a scowl on his face, a bedpan in his hands, and a hot dog sticking out from the breast pocket of his overcoat.

As he stomped across the room on the way to his office,

workers were thankful that their cubicles provided some protection from Bozeman's notoriously judgmental glare. One of those workers, a tall, frail man named Edison, did not duck behind his cubicle divider but instead walked quickly toward his boss as Bozeman headed to his office on the corner of the floor.

"Steve," said Edison with urgency. "I'm glad you're here. The Swinson brothers have been waiting in your office since eight thirty this morning."

Bozeman responded by thrusting the bedpan into Edison's bony chest. "Have this tested for fingerprints and DNA right away," he growled.

For a moment, Edison just stared at the rusty metal object. As the chief financial officer of Rainforest, he hadn't the foggiest idea how to test anything, especially a ruined bedpan, for DNA.

"Is this a bedpan, sir?" Edison asked, pushing his thick glasses back up the long bridge of his nose.

"No, it's a teapot," sniped Bozeman. "Why don't you brew yourself up a nice cup of Lemon Zinger?" He whipped out his cell phone and shoved the picture he had taken of Max under Edison's nose. "I want you to find out the identity of this assassin who attacked me while I was on my way to work with that very bedpan."

"Excuse me," said Edison, carefully taking the phone

from Bozeman. "But why were you on your way to work with a bedpan?"

"He *attacked* me with the bedpan," Bozeman snarled, pointing at the picture he'd snapped. "And I want you to hire me a couple of bodyguards. Big guys. And mean. The biggest and meanest you can find. Got it?"

Edison nodded and then watched as Bozeman removed the hot dog from his pocket, popped it between his teeth, then pulled out his silver-plated lighter and held the flame to the end of the frank.

"Excuse me, sir," said Edison. "You're . . . trying to smoke a hot dog."

When Bozeman realized his mistake, he snapped his lighter closed and angrily hurled the hot dog across the room, where it disappeared over a wall of cubicles and landed with an audible *sploosh*.

"Aaah!" came the sound of someone being burned by hot splashing coffee.

Bozeman ignored the scream and continued on toward his office. "I should warn you," said Edison as he struggled to keep pace with his boss. "The Swinson brothers are very unhappy with the last-minute changes to our offer."

Bozeman stopped at the door of his office, his fingers gripping the handle tightly enough that his knuckles turned white. "They're unhappy?" he said. "Well maybe we should bring in some balloons and a circus clown to cheer them up. And a pony."

With that, Bozeman's sneer morphed instantly into a big greasy smile as he turned the handle and pushed the door in. He marched into his office to find the Swinson brothers, Marty and Evan, putting on their jackets and collecting their things as if preparing to leave.

"Fellas!" said Bozeman, striding across the room directly toward Marty and right past his younger brother. Bozeman knew that Marty, an aging hippie, bald on top with a stark white ponytail that ran halfway down his back, was the one he needed to win over. Unlike his older brother, Evan was shy and reserved and he generally let Marty do the talking for the two of them.

"How are things?" Bozeman asked as he took Marty's hand, intentionally short-handing him (grabbing him by the fingers) and squeezing too hard.

"We're not happy, Steve," said Marty, straightening the jacket of his rumpled business suit that he'd paired with a well-wrinkled T-shirt and white high-top basketball shoes. "We've been waiting here for hours. We shouldn't have even needed to come in here. We had a deal." He pulled his squished fingers from Bozeman's oily grip.

"We still have a deal," said Bozeman. "It's just one tiny little change, that's all."

"Swinson Brothers Toys is more than a business," said Marty as his much-better-dressed younger brother nodded in agreement. "We're a family. Some of our people have been with us since the very beginning. And you're asking us to accept a deal that would put them out of work two weeks before Christmas?"

"Listen," said Bozeman. "I know exactly what you mean. I feel the same way about Rainforest. We're like one big happy family. Isn't that right, Edison?"

Edison appeared dumbfounded by the question. He barely managed to produce a tight smile as he muttered, "Uh . . . yes. Definitely . . . big. And . . . happy."

"So you see, I can appreciate your concerns here," said Bozeman. "But the fact remains that your toy stores have lost money for the last six quarters straight. It's time to face reality. You can either sell the company to me under the terms of the contract, or you can hold on to your quaint little mom-and-pop operation until you owe more money on it than it's worth and you show up for work one day to find a padlock on the front door."

Marty exhaled heavily and shared a pained look with Evan.

"The fact is," said Bozeman, "that toy stores are a thing of the past. The future, gentlemen, is Rainforest."

CHAPTER 6

THAT DOGGY IN THE WINDOW

Though a full hour had passed since Max's ill-fated bed-pan ride, he was still feeling a bit wobbly as he and his friends made their way through the busy midtown area.

Baxter, on the other hand, was still every bit as charged up as Max was shaken. "That was totally epic! Someday we'll be telling our grandkids about the day you sledded down 43rd Street."

"Yeah, if we live that long," said Max, stopping to steady himself against a lamppost. "I still feel like I'm gonna throw up." He leaned forward, resting his hands on his knees just in case.

"You've got your whole life to throw up," said Leoni.

"Come on. Let's find some more Christmasy stuff to do."

"Throwing up is actually pretty Christmasy at my house," said Baxter, explaining his mother's annual "tradition" of undercooking the turkey. "What do you guys want to do?"

"We could go over to Hinkleman's Toys and walk around and pretend we're gonna buy something," offered Leoni.

"Hinkleman's? Didn't you hear?" said Max. "It closed down. Couple weeks ago."

"They can't be closed!" Baxter gasped. "That was the last toy store in the neighborhood." He reached out and kicked the side of a brick building and then winced at the resulting pain.

"Everyone just buys toys online now, I guess," said Leoni. "Anyway, it doesn't really affect us all that much, since we can't afford to buy anything anyway."

"Doesn't affect me at all," said Max. "Because what I want for Christmas you won't find in a toy store anyway."

"Let me guess," said Leoni dryly. "World peace."

"A submarine," said Baxter.

"Not even close," said Max. "Come on. I'll show you."

Just six blocks away, in an old brick building, stood Jimmy O'Reilly's Pets. And in the window of that store, a woolly-faced Airedale terrier puppy sat up and put its front paws on the glass. The dog scratched excitedly at the sight of Max, which wasn't surprising given that he'd stopped by to visit the puppy every day for the past two weeks on his way home from school.

Max pressed his hand against the windowpane, and the dog made a very good effort to lick it.

"Well? What do you think?" said Max. "Pretty cool, huh? I already named him and everything. I call him Plato."

Baxter's nose wrinkled. "You named a dog after a lump of clay?"

"No," said Max. "Not Play-Doh! Plato."

"Ohhh," said Baxter. "*Play*-Doh."

Max tried once more. "Plato. The philosopher. I named him that because he's so smart. You can just see it in his eyes. He's going to be my Christmas present."

"Uh, I'm not sure how to put this," Baxter said with hesitation. "Santa travels in a sleigh, not an ark. He can't be delivering animals all over the world."

Max failed to see the logic. "Why not?"

"Because they'd be chewing up the seats and making a mess in the sleigh while Santa's trying to drive, that's why not."

Because Baxter was older and bigger and had defended Max against bullies on many occasions, Max held his friend's opinion in very high regard. "I never thought about that," he said.

"It's true," Baxter continued. "Santa doesn't do animals. Remember my monkey?"

"Oh yeah. That's right," said Max, sighing.

"Monkey?" said Leoni. "What monkey?"

"I've been asking Santa for a monkey every year since I was three," Baxter explained. "Seven years later, still no monkey. I'm telling you, Max, the only way you're gonna get that puppy for Christmas is if you buy it yourself or if the Plimptons buy it for you."

The Plimptons were Max's foster parents.

Max had lived with the Plimptons for almost three years now, and Max knew that they kept him around not because they were particularly fond of him or because he was quiet and easy to take care of, but because the Plimptons loved the money they got for housing Max, even though the Plimptons were by no means poor.

Walt Plimpton was a dentist, and dentists, as a general rule, make very good money. No, the Plimptons were not poor; they were just incredibly cheap. Max knew there was no chance that they would buy him a dog for Christmas, especially considering that last year they'd given him three sample-size bottles of mouthwash and a roll of gauze.

And, of course, the idea of Max buying the dog himself was absurd. With an allowance of twenty-five cents a week, by the time he had enough money, Plato would probably be seventy in dog years.

"It's just as well," Max said sadly. "They don't allow pets in my apartment building anyway."

He looked back at the pup, who still pawed frantically at the glass. It may have only been three-quarters of an inch thick, but as far as Max was concerned it might as well have been ten feet of granite. He put his hand to the glass once more and smiled weakly. "Goodbye, Plato," he said. "I'm sure someone will give you a nice home. I just hope they don't give you some boring name like Ranger or Scout."

Max was suddenly angry with himself. He should have known better than to have gotten his hopes up. He took one long last look at Plato, yipping silently behind the window. "Well," he said, his voice just above a whisper. "I should probably go home now and start on my chores."

"You have chores?" asked Leoni, shying away as if Max had just confessed he had worms. "What kind of chores?"

"Well, it's Tuesday, so I have to wash all the dental floss and hang it out to dry."

"You're kidding me," said Baxter.

"No," said Max. "You can't put it in the dryer because of the wax coating."

"That's gross," said Leoni. "How much money do your foster parents save by reusing dental floss?"

"Not enough to buy me a puppy," said Max.

CHAPTER 7

PIZZA RUN

It had only been two hours, but Skhiff's back was killing him and his hands had begun to develop blisters from all the shoveling. Eldor, on the other hand, had managed to avoid injury by doing nothing but resting his chin on the end of his shovel's handle.

"You know, usually the first person to do something is celebrated as a hero, with a bronze statue and a ticker-tape parade," he groused. "First man on the moon? Hero. First person to circumnavigate the globe? Hero. First guys to put pants on a moose? Losers, sentenced to a lifetime of shoveling animal poop."

"Yeah, speaking of which," said Skhiff sharply, "I'd

rather not shovel it all by myself, if you don't mind." He stopped to wipe the sweat from his brow. It wasn't easy to perspire at the North Pole in midwinter. He'd been working that hard.

"I'd love to help you out," said Eldor, "but I'm famished." Eldor flung his shovel to the ground with a *clang*. "And when Eldor gets low blood sugar, Eldor doesn't work until Eldor gets something to eat. And what Eldor wants to eat is authentic Italian thin-crust pizza."

When Eldor started to refer to himself in the third person—or, in this case, the third elf—Skhiff knew that trouble was not too far behind. He noticed that Eldor was looking toward the far end of the stable, where Santa's sleigh was parked beneath a large red tarp.

"You know what I love about Christmas?" asked Eldor as he walked slowly toward the sleigh. "It's a time of giving. And so I think it's time we gave ourselves a little Christmas present."

"Eldor? What are you doing?" said Skhiff, hurrying after him. "No, no."

Eldor began undoing the ties that held the tarp in place. "Come on, give me a hand," he said.

"You can't do this," Skhiff scolded. "You can't just take the sleigh for a joyride."

Eldor peeled back the tarp, revealing the sleigh and its glossy candy apple–red finish. "Why not? What do you have against joy, exactly?"

"Nothing. I think the record will show that I am very pro-joy. But Gnurk said . . ."

"Gnurk says a lot of things," Eldor retorted. "And usually the same things over and over again. Besides, no one's gonna find out. So are you in or not?"

"No," said Skhiff firmly. "I am not going to help you steal the sleigh. End of discussion."

"Let me ask you something," said Eldor as he began folding the heavy tarp. "Is it wrong to steal in order to feed your starving family?"

"Yeah, but we're not starving," said Skhiff.

"Speak for yourself," Eldor replied, pausing to pat his large soft belly. "So, what do you say? I'm buying."

Though the idea of authentic Italian thin-crust pizza was becoming more and more intriguing, there was still one big problem as Skhiff saw it. "But what about the Oath of Elves? We're not allowed to reveal ourselves to humans."

"We're not allowed to reveal ourselves as *elves*," Eldor corrected. "There's nothing to prevent us from revealing ourselves as, say, leprechauns."

"Leprechauns? What are you talking about?"

"Remember our costumes from last year's St. Patrick's Day party? That's the solution. We'll just pose as a couple of kids dressed up as leprechauns for Halloween. We'll blend right in."

"Halloween was six weeks ago," said Skhiff.

"We'll pose as kids dressed up as leprechauns for Halloween who got lost on their way home. Trust me, it'll work. Come on, whaddaya say? Sausage? Mushrooms? Black olives? And . . ."

"No. Don't say it," Skhiff warned, jabbing an index finger in Eldor's direction for emphasis. "Do not say it!"

"Spicy pepperoni!"

"Noooo." Skhiff clutched a pointy ear in each hand, fell to his knees, and wailed to the sky. "Spicy pepperoni. My one weakness."

"What are you talking about?" said Eldor. "You have a thousand weaknesses. And I know them all. Now let's go."

CHAPTER 8

THE PLIMPTONS

When Max walked into the lobby of the Plimptons' shabby old apartment building, he ran into one of his least favorite people in the world—the apartment manager, Mrs. Derooey. She was using a razor blade to remove bits of Scotch tape from the window.

"Hi, Mrs. Derooey," said Max, hurrying past on his way to the elevator.

"Hold on there, young man," she spat back. "What exactly is this?" Her sketched-on eyebrows sloped downward, and she flattened out a crumpled piece of paper and held it up for Max's inspection.

The handwritten notice read, "Wanted: Used

Toothbrushes," with a phone number scrawled underneath.

"I assume this was put up by your parents," Mrs. Derooey snarled. "I don't know of anyone else cheap enough to use a toothbrush that someone else has had in their mouth."

"Well, you boil them first," explained Max, while rapidly pushing the button on the elevator. "And actually they're my foster parents."

"I don't care if they're your half parents, twice removed," said Mrs. Derooey. "I have spoken to Walt and Noreena on numerous occasions about this. There are to be no flyers of any kind posted in the lobby at any time. That's the rule, and all rules must be followed. No flyers, no smoking, no pets, and . . . are you chewing gum?"

"What? No," said Max, quickly swallowing the piece of gum he'd been chewing.

"Good. Now you tell your parents that they've had their last warning. One more violation of the rules and they're out of here. Got it?"

"Yes, ma'am," said Max, relieved that the elevator had finally shown up.

On the fourth floor, Max walked down the hallway, over the bumpy gray carpet toward the Plimptons' apartment. When he walked in, he was not the least bit surprised to see Mrs. Plimpton wearing woolen mittens and a thick turtleneck sweater while sitting at the kitchen table and furiously clipping coupons from stacks of newspapers retrieved from the neighbors' recycling bins.

In their never-ending campaign to cut costs, the Plimptons kept their apartment dimly lit and heated to something far below what most people would consider room temperature.

"You're late," said Mrs. Plimpton, without looking up from her clipping. With each word, a puff of steam rose into the cold air from her bright-red lips, waxy from the old crayons she used as lipstick.

"Sorry," said Max. "I lost track of time."

"As long as you get those chores done."

"Don't worry, I will," said Max. "I just have to use the bathroom first."

"Remember," said Mrs. Plimpton in a singsongy voice, "*if it's yellow let it stew, we only flush for number two. We can't be wasting water, you know.*"

"Right," said Max, who was glad the Plimptons kept the temperature low in an apartment where the toilet was rarely flushed.

He quickly tended to his Tuesday chores, using a broken broom handle to swirl the used floss around in a bucket of soapy water before rinsing it and hanging it, strand by strand, over the shower curtain rod to dry.

Max finished the task just in time for dinner. Tonight was Mrs. Plimpton's famous spaghetti and meatball, because as Dr. Plimpton would say, "One meatball should be enough for one family." In addition, Dr. Plimpton, a thin, undernourished man, had returned from work with everything needed for a salad, boasting that he had even procured some free croutons by being "faster than those lazy ducks at the park."

Max watched as Mrs. Plimpton ladled some sauce made of warm water and ketchup packets onto his pasta. Then she placed the well-used paper plate before him and sat down across from her gaunt husband.

"So how was work today?" she asked.

"Fantastic," said Dr. Plimpton, removing a handful of coins from his pocket. "I discovered that if I just tilt the chair back at a slightly greater angle, a lot more spare change spills out of people's pockets. Look. Two dollars and twenty-seven cents."

"Brilliant!" beamed Mrs. Plimpton, admiring the sampling of coins as if they were the Crown Jewels.

After dinner, Max retired to his room. Upon entering, he did what he always did first: he said hello to the photo of his mother, resting on the cardboard banana box that served as his nightstand.

The photo was of the two of them together, smiling joyously while the Statue of Liberty stood proudly in the background. It was from his mother that Max got his sense of adventure.

"Everything is in motion," Max remembered her telling him one night as they lay upon a blanket in Central Park, staring up at the night sky until well past his bedtime. "All the parts of the universe are moving. All you have to do is jump on and go for a ride."

That trip to New York City was supposed to have been the first of many adventures they would share. It was a warm-up for a Paris trip for which his mom had been saving for years. It was number one on the list of all the places she wanted to see.

But everything changed in the blink of an eye and with the changing of a yellow light to red, which a man driving a delivery van failed to notice. And though the accident happened three years ago, Max still sometimes felt sure that one day his mother would knock on the door and whisk him off to Paris and far away from the Plimptons and their cold, dark, smelly apartment.

CHAPTER 9

A GIFT FROM ABOVE

"What did I tell you?" yelled Eldor over the roar of the winter wind. Though he had never flown a reindeer-powered sleigh before, it seemed to come naturally to him. He was in complete control as the friends cut through the dim and foggy late-afternoon sky.

"This is amazing," Skhiff agreed, and tore into another slice. "And I thought you had to go all the way to Italy to get authentic Italian thin-crust pizza. Who knew?"

"What I do know is that you can take that beard off now," said Eldor of the orange leprechaun beard stuck to Skhiff's chin, now caked in pizza sauce and crust crumbs.

"It's okay," Skhiff responded. "It keeps my chin warm.

You know, when I'm old enough, I think I might try growing one of these."

"Hey, spot me a slice, would you?" said Eldor with a nod toward the pizza box that rested on the seat behind him.

Skhiff flipped open the box, and when he did the wind took hold of the lid and scooped the entire box into the air. In a split second, to Skhiff's utter horror, the pizza—cheese, sauce, crust, and all—scattered to the wind, and immediately eight reindeer went after the six slices. The sleigh pitched and reeled, while Eldor tugged hard on the reins, fighting to keep it under control.

"No!" Eldor yelled. "Bad reindeer! Bad! Stop it!"

The reindeer paid Eldor no mind, even as the sleigh went into a steep dive. Skhiff's face turned as green as the leprechaun hat that covered his pointy ears. "I think I'm going to throw up," he announced.

"You've got your whole life to throw up," Eldor shouted. "Right now I need you to help me pull!"

Skhiff gathered himself and gripped the reins tightly, and he and Eldor pulled back as hard as was elfinly possible until the sleigh finally began to level off.

"Whew, that was close," said Skhiff, wiping sweat from his brow.

"Relax," said Eldor. "We're dressed as leprechauns. We're good luck. What could possibly go wrong?"

No sooner had Eldor uttered these words than Skhiff's eyes widened. "Eldor" was all he could say while pointing dead ahead.

It should be noted that reindeer, like bats, possess a kind of radar that normally would have detected the large steel-and-glass structure that had just emerged out of the mist. This early-warning system, however, can apparently be short-circuited when the reindeer's brains are occupied by thoughts of falling pizza.

"Swerve!" yelled Eldor. Together he and Skhiff tugged as hard as they could at the reins. The sleigh banked sharply to the right. The reindeer came within inches of hitting the radio tower topping the skyscraper, but the sleigh trailed behind and inches lower and slammed into the radio tower with a *crunch*, a *clang*, and enough force to cause the sleigh's trunk to pop open.

"I don't believe it!" yelled Skhiff, burying his face in his hands. "'What could possibly go wrong?' he says. 'We're dressed as leprechauns.'"

"Don't sweat it, my vertically challenged little friend,"

said Eldor, reaching back to slam the open trunk shut. "It's just a scratch. We just have to get this baby back under the tarp as soon as we get home. And the sooner we get home, the better."

As Eldor took the sleigh up to a higher cruising altitude, neither he nor Skhiff suspected for a second that the big red bag stored in the trunk had fallen out and was now drifting down toward the ground.

And the elves certainly couldn't have imagined that Max, Baxter, and Leoni would be directly below, after having spent yet another day of Christmas break searching for something to do.

"Maybe tomorrow we could go down to the river and skip rocks," Baxter suggested as the three friends walked through their colorless neighborhood, where dumpsters overflowed and thick weeds poked up from beneath the dirty snow.

"The river's frozen," Leoni replied.

"Yeah, like my toes," said Max. "Maybe we can think of something to do indoors for a change."

"Yeah, but what can you do indoors that doesn't cost money?" asked Leoni.

Before anyone could answer, they were startled by a dull

thud, as something resembling a large pile of mud landed on the hood of a parked car.

"Wow," said Baxter over the blaring of the car's alarm. The three moved in for a closer look. "The pigeons in this city are really out of control."

"Yeah," Leoni agreed. "That's the biggest poop I've ever seen. And I have two older brothers."

A second later, Baxter lost all interest in the thought of oversize pigeons when several pieces of pizza landed at his feet. "It's a miracle," he gasped in amazement at the sight of it.

"Is that pizza?" asked Max.

Baxter bent down, picked it up, and brushed off the slush. "It sure is," he said, flicking a few tiny rocks and bits of dirt off its surface.

"You're not going to eat that, are you?" asked Leoni.

Baxter looked at Leoni like she was crazy for questioning his willingness to eat food off the ground. "Why not?" he said with a shrug.

"Because you don't know where it came from, that's why not."

A connoisseur of pizza, burritos, hamburgers, and of all things fast food, Baxter took a huge bite and chewed thoughtfully for a few moments before saying, "Corsoni's on 85th. That's where it came from. I can tell by the sauce."

"Yeah, but how did it get here?" asked Max, searching the skies directly overhead.

"Don't know," said Baxter as he took another bite. "Don't care."

"My stepdad took me to a basketball game once," said Leoni. "They shot T-shirts into the crowd with a special cannon."

"Are you saying that was shot out of a pizza cannon?" said Max.

"Makes about as much sense as anything else," answered Leoni.

Everyone took a moment to consider this when, all of a sudden, a large bright-red bag, open side down, landed on Max's head.

Surprised to find himself in complete darkness, Max grappled with the bag while his two friends stood by, laughing hysterically.

"Oh man, you should see your hair right now." Baxter laughed when Max finally managed to wrest the bag from his head and throw it to the ground.

"You sure taught that bag a lesson," Leoni snickered.

"It's not funny," said Max, looking at the bag resting near his feet. He gave it an angry kick. When the bag did nothing but lie there like a giant deflated cloth balloon, Max bent down and cautiously picked it up.

"Oh. It's just a bag," said Max, giving it a good shake. "A big red bag. Okay. Cool."

"Cool?" With a sniff, Baxter showed how unimpressed he was. "What's so cool about it? Can't eat it." He took another bite of pizza and spat out a pebble.

"Well, I like it," said Leoni. "What are you gonna do with it?"

"Don't know," said Max, inspecting every inch of the bag, checking for holes or other defects and finding none. "Maybe I'll cut it up and make a shirt out of it. The Plimptons haven't bought me new clothes in almost two years."

"What? That's horrible," gasped Leoni.

"Tell me about it," said Max. "If my tighty-whities get any tighter my legs are gonna go numb."

CHAPTER 10

THE MAGIC BAG

Before entering the apartment building, Max carefully folded the red bag and stuffed it under his coat for fear that Mrs. Plimpton would find some money-saving use for it or that Mrs. Derooey might have some weird rule about having large cloth sacks inside.

As he walked past Mrs. D's office door, he could hear her yelling into the phone.

"This is the fourth time you've failed to clean the lint trap on the dryer in the laundry room, Mrs. Fleming. You do realize it could cause a fire and burn down the whole building. And if that happens, it's going to come right out of your damage deposit."

When Max walked into his apartment and found no one home, he was reminded that today was Wednesday, the day that Mrs. Plimpton went to the blood bank to sell her blood.

"It's twenty dollars and a free doughnut," she would say.

On Wednesdays, Max's chores included picking out all the pennies from the change that Dr. Plimpton had retrieved from the crease of his dental chair and using a ball-peen hammer to flatten them out so that they would fit into the quarter slots at the laundromat. After that, he was expected to scrub clean a jar full of teeth that Dr. Plimpton had pulled from his patients' heads so he could use them to make dentures, essentially selling their own teeth back to them.

But today, Max did not feel much like doing chores. Exhausted from wandering around looking for something to do, he walked directly to his bedroom. He said hello to the photo of his mother, then removed the red bag from beneath his coat. He stuffed it under the bed, which was shoved against the wall of the tiny room that he had decorated with photos of all the places he and his mother had planned to visit together. There were photos of the Grand Canyon, Machu Picchu, the Taj Mahal, Buckingham Palace, and many others, all clipped from travel magazines that Mrs. Plimpton had collected from the recycling.

Max plopped down onto the bed and grabbed a catalog from the now-defunct Hinkleman's Toys that had been resting on the nightstand since the last time he and his friends had gone there. He lay back and began thumbing through the curled pages of the flyer.

"Well, if I can't have a puppy, it might as well be toys," he muttered, hoping that Santa would be far less stingy than the Plimptons had been. "Okay, I've gotta narrow it down to my top ten. Definitely the skateboard. And that bike is awesome. The USA Hockey for sure. Oh, and a foosball table, and the remote-control battle tank. Basketball hoop, of course. And the Captain Lightning action set. And . . ."

Suddenly Max's bed started to move—not across the room but upward, rising like a loaf of bread in the oven. He dropped the flyer and clutched at his blanket as the bed rumbled and rose higher yet. "Earthquake," he said to himself. "Wait a minute. Do we have earthquakes here?"

Another series of jolts lifted the bed until it was now a good two feet higher than it had been. "Oh no," whispered Max, who had seen more horror movies than he should have at his age. "I must be possessed—or my bed is."

Afraid to move, he just lay there, paralyzed, until he heard a strange but familiar sound. It was eerily similar to

the sound of a toy battle tank he had recently test-driven at Hinkleman's. And, as he turned his head slowly and glanced over the edge of the bed, there it was, that very same tank, buzzing slowly across the room until it collided with his dresser.

Max carefully slipped off his now-wobbly bed, grabbed the toy tank, and quickly shut it off. When he turned back, he covered his mouth to stifle what would have otherwise been a scream. A brand-new basketball rolled out from the darkness underneath.

"Okay," whispered Max. "Now this is getting weird."

He lowered himself to his hands and knees and peered under the bed. There he saw the red bag, which was no longer neatly folded and no longer empty. In fact, it was practically bursting at the seams with toys. And not just any toys. When Max dragged the bag out from under the bed and began emptying its contents onto the floor, he soon realized that he was now in the presence of every toy he had added to his list. They were all there—the bicycle, the hockey table, the skateboard. All of them.

"I don't believe it," Max murmured. "It gave me everything I asked for." One might think that the idea would occur to him right away, but it took a good couple of minutes before Max's eyes brightened and he looked at the bag and said, "A puppy. I want a puppy."

His heart nearly exploded with joy when he heard a faint barking coming from inside the bag. Max took a deep breath and carefully lifted the edge of the bag and peered inside, only to be greeted by a very realistic, but still mechanical, yapping toy dog.

He picked up the dog and looked it over. Not exactly what he'd had in mind. "A toy puppy," he said sadly. "Looks like the bag only makes toys." Almost instantly, Max realized the absurdity of such a statement. "What am I saying? It's a bag that makes toys! Toys! This is unbelievable! Baxter and Leoni are gonna freak!"

CHAPTER 11

NO LIMIT

Though it had served as a sledding hill just a few days before, the condemned house more regularly operated as a fort that frequently had to be defended from imaginary intruders of all kinds.

In the room that had once been the kitchen, Baxter looked out the window through a rusted tailpipe he'd found. "Alien ship approaching at warp nine," he said in his most captain-like voice. "Prepare to launch the Widow Maker!"

"Aye-aye, Captain," Leoni shouted from the living room of the fort, which was cluttered with street signs, road cones, and other discarded items the three friends had found. An old, bent-up basketball hoop hung crookedly on the wall, where Leoni had nailed it. A ratty recliner that Baxter had found on the side of the road was now suspended from the ceiling by a collection of cables and bungee cords that they'd salvaged. It was the only swing in town with a cup holder and a retractable footrest.

It had been Max's idea to nail a bicycle inner tube to the frame of the glassless kitchen window to create a giant slingshot, which Leoni was now loading with an old paint can full of mud, leaves, and garbage. She pulled back on the inner tube, grunting as she stretched it to its limit. "Widow Maker ready, Captain!"

"And . . . fire!" said Baxter.

Leoni released the inner tube, and the paint can shot across the front yard, colliding with an old, long-dead oak tree with a wonderfully destructive *clang*.

"Nice shot," came a voice from behind Leoni.

She turned to see Max standing there. He was holding the red bag, neatly folded once more. "Where have you been?" she asked. "I thought we were meeting here at nine."

"Yeah," said Baxter, walking in from the kitchen. "You're missing all the fun."

"Oh . . . the fun is just beginning," said Max, and he

shook the bag out to its full length. "Check this out," he said with a wry smile.

"Yeah, we see it," said Baxter. "It's that crummy old bag again."

"Yeah," said Leoni. "Super exciting. We can have a lot of fun with that bag. Hey, maybe we could, I don't know, put stuff in it."

"Yeah, and then take the stuff back out again," said Baxter. "I could do that all day."

"Make fun all you want," said Max. "But if you could have one thing for Christmas, anything at all, what would it be?"

Leoni looked at Baxter, then back at Max. This exercise seemed pointless. Like most of the kids she knew, what Leoni wanted for Christmas and what she got were often two very different things. "I don't know." She shrugged. "A new baseball glove, I guess. A real leather one."

"Okay," said Max. "How about you, Bax?"

Baxter took a moment to consider this. "Besides a monkey? I guess I'd like a fake moustache. Then I could be a master of disguise."

Max's friends watched with wrinkled brows as he opened the bag and spoke directly into it. "Okay," he said. "I want a genuine real leather baseball glove and a genuine fake moustache." Baxter's and Leoni's concern soon turned to amazement when Max reached deep into the bag and retrieved those exact two items.

"Whoa," said Baxter. "A fake moustache. Okay—mind officially blown. How'd you do that?"

"Magic," said Max as he tossed the glove to Leoni, then peeled the adhesive strip off the back of the moustache and slapped it onto Baxter's forehead, giving him an instant fake unibrow.

"Hey," Baxter objected.

"You stole this stuff and hid it in that bag," said Leoni.

"I didn't steal it," Max snapped. "The bag made it."

"Hey, this is stuck," said Baxter, tugging at the moustache on his forehead.

"Oh, the bag *made* it," said Leoni, her voice dripping with sarcasm. "Riiight. Well that certainly explains everything."

"It's true," Max insisted. "All I have to do is ask it for something and it just appears in the bag."

"Okay," said Baxter, still trying to remove the moustache. "Ask it for a ham sandwich. With mustard."

"And some chocolate milk," Leoni added.

"No, it doesn't make food," Max explained. "Or puppies. I already tried."

"How about fake-moustache remover?" asked Baxter.

"Nope," said Max. "It only makes toys." He folded the bag in half and tossed it to Leoni. "Here. Try it. Ask for any toy you can think of."

Leoni took the bag, and Max reached out and tore the mustache from Baxter's forehead along with a significant portion of Baxter's eyebrows.

"Ow!"

"Okay," said Leoni, ignoring Baxter's cry. "I'll play along." She opened the bag, peered inside, and spoke to it.

"Hello in there. Uh . . . give me an archery set, a stunt bike, and a set of really nice golf clubs for my stepdad." Leoni stared into the bag, her skepticism growing with each second that passed with no results. "Magic bag," she scoffed. "Now tell us where you really got this stuff."

"I want an archery set, a stunt bike, and a set of really nice golf clubs," Max rattled off, and almost instantly the bag expanded. Leoni struggled under the increasing weight of it and fell backward with a clatter. The suddenly full bag was splayed across her chest. "I . . . can't . . . get up," she uttered.

Together Max and Baxter dragged the bag off their friend, and then Max pulled an archery set, a stunt bike, and a set of what appeared to be really nice golf clubs out of the bag for his friends to see.

Stunned silence filled the room until Leoni finally whispered, "This is the greatest discovery in the history of humankind."

Baxter snatched the empty bag from the floor. "Yes, and now it's my turn," he announced. "Give me a Super Soaker."

Excitedly, he reached deep into the bag, plunging his entire head inside. He reemerged seconds later with nothing but a baffled look.

"Give me a Super Soaker," Max said in the direction of the bag. "There. Now try it."

Baxter peered into the bag once more and there it was—a Super Soaker. "I don't get it," Baxter said, pulling the toy from the bag. "How come it only works for you?"

Max shrugged. "I don't know. Must be like the genie in the magic lamp. Because I'm the one who found it, I'm like its master or something."

A look of panic suddenly washed over Baxter's face. "Oh no," he muttered.

"What?" said Leoni. "What's wrong?"

"If it's like the magic lamp, maybe there's a limited number of times you can wish for stuff.

Maybe this will all come to an end." By now Baxter was very close to hyperventilating.

"Take it easy," said Max. "If there is a limited amount of stuff we can get from the bag, we might as well find out right now and get it over with."

"How are we gonna do that?" asked Leoni.

"Easy," said Max, focusing once more on the bag. "Give me a million LEGOs."

For a moment, nothing happened. It was almost as if the bag were taking a deep breath. Then, with a rushing, rumbling, rolling crescendo, an avalanche of LEGOs poured from the bag. Max and his friends watched with delight as tiny plastic blocks cascaded from the bag like water over a burst dam. They tried to run but were swept away by the colorful tsunami.

When the noise finally stopped, the sea of bricks filled the fort to the point that the three friends were completely submerged below the sea of tiny plastic blocks.

Like a zombie rising up from the grave, Max's hand shot out from the pile of LEGOs, followed soon after by his head. He looked out across the room and breathed a sigh of relief when he spotted Baxter and Leoni fighting their way to the surface of the pile as well. For a moment the three friends just stared at each other, shoulder-deep in LEGOs. Then Max looked at the others and smiled. "There's no limit!"

CHAPTER 12

THE AWFUL TRUTH

It was day two of shoveling manure and Eldor and Skhiff had, as a result, worked up quite an appetite. And, as they would discover, one of the best ways to get lots of dirty looks is to go out to eat when you smell strongly of reindeer poop.

The other elves coughed and waved at the air as the two stinky stablehands walked through the cafeteria, their trays piled high with cake, cookies, candy canes, and large bowls of whipped cream.

The two friends sat at a long table that was apparently not nearly long enough for the two lady elves already sitting there. Theela and Avette immediately slid down the bench, as far away from Eldor and Skhiff as possible.

"Okay," said Theela, looking as if she had just eaten a lemon. "No offense, but did something die on you?"

"What? Oh, that." Eldor chuckled as he gave his sleeve a quick sniff. "No, nothing died on us. It's reindeer manure, so technically it's still alive, I think. You know, with all the germs and bacteria and stuff."

In perfect unison, Theela and Avette dropped their forks and pushed their trays away. For them, lunch just ended early.

"Sorry about that," said Skhiff. "Could we make it up to you by buying you a dessert of your choice?"

"Yeah," said Eldor, leaning over and shoving his plate under Theela's nose. "Or, better yet, help yourself to one of my cookies."

While Theela just stared at the offering in disgust and disbelief, Avette was taking a closer look at their uninvited dining companions.

"There's something familiar about you guys," she said. "Is it possible I've seen—or maybe smelled—you somewhere before?"

"It's entirely possible," Eldor replied with a chuckle. "We're the guys who put the pants on the moose." Eldor turned and fist-bumped Skhiff.

"Oh, right," said Theela, her squint softening into a look

of bemusement. "I read about it in the *North Pole News*. Very, uh . . . clever."

"Clever," said Eldor. "That's us in a nutshell. The name's Eldor. This is my partner in crime, Skhiff. How about you two? Haven't seen you around before."

"We just graduated from Elf Academy," said Avette. "We work at the head office."

"Head office," Eldor repeated with a nod of approval. "Nice."

"Yeah, in fact we really need to get back," said Theela as she and Avette stood up and grabbed their trays. "Big meeting this afternoon about the missing toys."

"Missing toys?" asked Skhiff. "What missing toys?"

"Seriously? Everyone's talking about it," Avette scoffed. "About a million LEGOS. Along with a bunch of other stuff." Then she reached into her purse and pulled out two pine tree air fresheners and handed one each to Eldor and Skhiff. "Here. These are for you."

"A Christmas present?" Eldor beamed.

"Yes. For the rest of us."

Eldor and Skhiff gave the air fresheners a sniff as Avette and Theela hurried out of the room as if it were on fire.

"Well?" said Skhiff. "What do you think?"

"Lovely pine scent," said Eldor.

"No, I mean about the missing toys."

"Yeah, terrible," said Eldor. "Crime is really out of control."

"There is no crime here," said Skhiff. "There's only one way for toys to leave the North Pole, and that's with the bag."

"Yeah, but the bag is in the trunk of the sleigh, right where we left it," said Eldor with a dismissive wave.

"Okay," said Skhiff. "But if memory serves me correctly, didn't the trunk sort of pop open when we hit that radio tower?"

"Hmm," said Eldor, no longer sounding so dismissive. "Maybe we should, uh . . ."

"Yeah, we definitely should," Skhiff agreed.

In a sudden panic the two elves raced from the cafeteria and across the plaza to the stables, where they frantically tore the tarp off the sleigh and opened the dented trunk. But all they found were a couple of roadside flares that Santa kept for emergency situations.

"Noooo!" wailed Skhiff, tightly gripping the points of his ears until they went numb. "It's gone. This is horrible. Absolutely horrible." Skhiff turned and began banging his forehead against the stable wall. "I can't believe it. I can't believe I let you talk me into taking the sleigh for a joyride."

"Hey," said Eldor, placing a hand on Skhiff's shoulder. "Don't blame yourself."

"Myself?" blared Skhiff, straightening up and taking Eldor by the lapels of his jacket. "I'm not blaming myself. I'm blaming *you*. It's always your fault. The potato salad man, exploding toys, pants on a moose! They're all your ridiculous ideas."

As calmly as he could, Eldor pointed to Skhiff's fists, which were full of Eldor's jacket. "Violence? Really?" he said, shaking his head sadly. "Is this what it's come to?"

Skhiff sighed and released Eldor with a sharp shove, then began pacing and squeezing his ears. "I'm sorry. I just really don't want to live in Greenland, okay?"

"No one's going to Greenland," said Eldor. "Relax, would you? Haven't I always looked out for you?"

"No. As a matter of fact, you have not," said Skhiff.

"Check it out," said Eldor. He took Skhiff by the elbow, escorted him to the door of the stable and pointed to the center of the square, where an eight-foot-tall jumbotron screen displayed a digital countdown to Christmas Eve. "We've still got six days, three hours, seven minutes, and fourteen seconds. Thirteen, twelve, eleven . . ."

"Stop! Stop counting! You're wasting time."

"Exactly," replied Eldor calmly. "I can afford to waste

time, because we've got plenty of it. Trust me. Finding the bag will be a piece of cake. All we have to do is retrace our steps."

"You'd better be right," said Skhiff. "Still, there's one thing I don't get. The bag only works for Santa. So why is it still transporting toys?"

Eldor shrugged. "When we find it, we can ask it. The important thing is we get it back, or there will be no Christmas this year."

"And we'll be polar bear food," Skhiff added.

Eldor nodded in agreement, then turned to his right, where the reindeer were resting in their individual stalls. "Okay, let's get 'em harnessed up and hit the road."

"No way," said Skhiff. "We are not taking the sleigh out again."

"Fine, suit yourself," said Eldor. "Then we'll have to go by reindeer. The question is, which of these four-legged poop factories should we take?"

"Dasher's the fastest," Skhiff offered.

"Dasher it is, then," said Eldor making a beeline for Dasher's stall.

"Of course he's also the biggest jerk," Skhiff called out.

Eldor scoffed and rolled his eyes as he unlatched the gate. "It's all a matter of showing the beast who's boss. Just call me the reindeer whisperer."

Eldor never got a chance to show off his skills, because the moment he walked behind Dasher the animal took the opportunity to use its hind legs to kick the unsuspecting elf right through the wall of the stable.

"Eldor!" Skhiff shouted as he ran to the elf-shaped hole in the wall. Peering through, he could see his friend lying motionless on the ground, surrounded by splinters of wood and flat on his back as if preparing to make a snow angel. "Eldor, are you okay?"

With all his remaining strength, Eldor managed to lift his head a few inches off the frozen ground. "You know, the good thing about internal bleeding is that it doesn't stain your clothes. And I'm thinking maybe we should go with Blitzen."

CHAPTER 13

TOYS ARE MONEY

It had taken up the better part of the morning, but the project was now complete. Built for style, not for comfort, a brand-new LEGO couch sat proudly in the living room of the fort, next to a matching LEGO easy chair (which, as you might imagine, was not terribly comfortable) and a LEGO coffee table. What remained of the million blocks had been swept into piles to the edges of the room in order to create enough space for the kind of fun that can only be had with an unlimited number of toys.

Baxter stood on the plastic couch and flew a remote-control plane around the room while Leoni did her best to knock it from the air by throwing Frisbees at it.

When she finally hit the plane, it crashed into the hundreds of plastic soldiers, superhero action figures, and model trucks and cars that they'd set up around the room.

"Yes!" said Leoni with a pump of her fist. "Take that."

"Hey, Max, I'm gonna need a new plane," Baxter called up. Max was standing on the landing above them.

"Sure," he said. "No problem." Without hesitation, he turned the bag upside down, held it over the staircase railing, and dumped a hundred Barbie dolls directly onto Baxter's head. "Aaah!" Baxter screamed, covering his head and falling to the floor. "Get 'em off me. I have a reputation to maintain."

"I'll get them off you," said Leoni, pelting Baxter with Nerf darts until he was forced to beg for mercy.

"Stop! I surrender." He giggled. He sat up and wiped tears of laughter from his eyes and yanked a Nerf dart from under his coat. "I can't believe it. This is easily the most fun I've ever had."

Leoni agreed, but Max was quiet. He just stood next to her, staring at the bag.

"What is it, Max?" she asked. "What's wrong?"

"It's weird," he replied. "I don't even have to say what I want anymore. I just think it, and there it is in the bag."

"You better watch out, then," said Baxter, brushing

Barbie dolls aside as he climbed to his feet. "Could turn out to be an evil bag."

"Evil?" said Max.

"Yeah, you know. Like in the movies. It starts out by giving you toys, but pretty soon you start thinking about sharp knives and meat cleavers and they come shooting out of the bag and chop your head off."

Max considered this for a moment. "Right. Well, there's only one way to find out." Baxter and Leoni winced as Max opened the bag and shouted, "Meat cleaver," then dove headfirst into the bag.

"Aaah!" came a muffled scream from the bag as Max twitched violently and rolled around on the floor before coming to a sudden stop at Baxter's feet where he lay motionless.

Baxter let out a nervous chuckle and casually stepped behind Leoni. "Ha-ha, Max. Real funny."

"Yeah, hilarious," said Leoni. "Now knock it off." She inched forward and gave Max's leg a nudge with her foot. She and Baxter were equally relieved when Max sat up suddenly.

"You jerk," said Baxter with a long exhale of relief. He reached out and grabbed the bag and yanked it from Max's head, then shrieked at what he saw. Max's face was mangled, bloody and unrecognizable. An evil chuckle somehow escaped Max's lips even though they weren't moving.

Once she'd gotten a better look, Leoni smiled, then took hold of the rubber zombie mask and yanked it off Max's head.

"You have to admit," said Max, still laughing, "that was a pretty good trick."

Leoni tossed the mask aside. "It sure was. I thought Baxter was gonna pee his pants."

"Yeah, but I didn't," said Baxter, a little too defensively. "Not even a little bit. You know, I should probably go home now. It's getting late."

"It's ten thirty in the morning," said Leoni. "And they'll dry out. Come on, you can't go home now. We've got a magic bag that makes toys."

"Okay," said Baxter. "I'll stay."

"You'd better. We're the luckiest kids in the whole world."

"I guess most people would think so," said Max, standing up and staring out the glassless window in the direction of Jimmy O'Reilly's Pets. "But to be honest, I'd trade all the toys in the world to be able to have that dog."

"I thought you said your apartment building doesn't allow dogs," said Baxter.

"If I could get that dog," said Max, "I'd find a way to make it work."

Leoni gave her chin a couple of tugs. "Then why don't you?" she said.

"Why don't I what?"

"You have a bag that makes toys," said Leoni. "Toys are worth money. Money can be exchanged for things like food, clothing . . ."

"And puppies," shouted Max. He spun away from the window, his eyes suddenly full of spark.

"And puppies," echoed Leoni, throwing Max a high five.

"Leoni, you are a genius," Max beamed, wrapping his friend up in a bear hug.

"What about me?" asked Baxter.

"You?" said Max over Leoni's shoulder. "You need to go home and change your pants."

CHAPTER 14

HALF THE PRICE

As Max and his friends would quickly realize, there are plenty of things to consider when opening up a business. There are the issues of what to call your business, how much to charge for your product, and, perhaps most important of all, location.

It was Leoni's idea to open up shop right in front of the old Hinkleman building. People unaware that the old toy store had recently shut down might still go there looking for presents, and now, rather than going home disappointed, they could still get anything they needed for half the price of buying it online.

The half-price idea was Leoni's, too. These days everyone

has a phone, so customers could simply look up the toy they wanted on the Rainforest website, then show the results to the highly trained staff at MBL Discount Toys (the name was Baxter's idea) and they'd sell them the item at exactly half that price.

"Not only that, there will be no shipping or handling costs," said Leoni as the three friends walked toward the former home of Hinkleman's. Max had the bag slung over his shoulder, and Baxter carried an old three-legged folding card table that they'd taken from the fort. Leoni had grabbed an old bedsheet to use as a tablecloth and a long stick to substitute for the table's fourth leg.

"I don't get that," said Baxter. "Why do they always say shipping *and* handling, anyway? I mean you can't really ship it without handling it, right?"

"Yeah," Max agreed. "And what if I don't want my stuff handled? Can I just pay for the shipping and not the handling?"

"Or just the handling and not the shipping?" said Baxter.

"You guys are weird," said Leoni just as they rounded a corner and Hinkleman's old store came into view.

It was a sad sight, to be sure. For as long as Max could remember, Hinkleman's had been a place where he and his friends could go to kill a few hours. They'd pretend to be interested in buying toys until Old Man Hinkleman would catch on and kick them out.

Leoni, however, was not in the mood for nostalgia. She grabbed the card table from Baxter and began snapping the folding legs into position on the sidewalk in front of the store. "Hinkleman's is the past now," she said as she flipped the table up onto its three legs, then jammed the stick in the place of the missing one. "MBL Discount Toys is the future."

She threw the old sheet over the table, then turned to Max. "You got the sign?"

Max replied by holding the red bag over the table and dumping out a small pile of alphabet building blocks. Leoni quickly lined up the blocks to read, "MBL Discount Toys. Pay less, play more."

"Not a bad slogan, if I do say so myself," she said while fine-tuning the arrangement of wooden blocks. "Okay, gentlemen. We are officially in business. I will be the marketing director, and Max will be the executive in charge of manufacturing."

"What about me?" asked Baxter. "What will I be?"

"You will be hiding under the table, taking stuff from the bag, and handing it to Max as required," said Leoni.

"Oh," said Baxter. "Does it have a title, at least?"

"Sure," said Leoni. "Your official title is warehouse superintendent."

Baxter considered this for a moment with a slow nod. "Okay," he said finally. "I just wanted to make sure I'm getting the same level of respect as everyone else."

"Of course you are," said Max. "Now get under the table."

When Baxter had positioned himself on the cold sidewalk next to the big red bag, Leoni, marketing director of MBL Discount Toys, went to work drumming up business.

"Excuse me, sir," she called out to a thin man in a business suit, walking while staring intently at his phone. "All your toy needs right here at half the price."

The man failed to so much as glance up and kept walking.

The next person to pass by was a heavyset woman lugging several department store shopping bags.

"Pardon me, ma'am," said Max. "Get your discount toys right here. Half the price of Rainforest, guaranteed."

This time the woman at least acknowledged their presence but only with a quick and suspicious gaze.

"What's with people today?" asked Leoni as the woman continued lumbering down the sidewalk.

"Yeah," said Max. "It's almost as if they have some

objection to buying invisible toys from a couple of strange kids on the street."

"You make a good point," said Leoni. "We need a nice little display. You know, with some variety."

"Got it," said Max. He quickly thought of a toy dump truck, a remote-control helicopter, a couple of toy ponies with long, unnaturally colored hair, and a few stuffed animals.

The items appeared in the bag, and Baxter handed them up to Max, who arranged them neatly behind the building blocks.

"Hey," said Baxter. "Can you make an extra teddy bear for me to sit on? My butt's getting cold."

The bag responded, and Baxter reached in and pulled out the requested item. "Pink?" Baxter scoffed. "Gee, thanks."

He wedged the fluffy pink bear between the cold sidewalk and his frozen backside just as the first customer of the day approached the table.

She was an eight-year-old girl who looked shy and just a little afraid.

"Hi," said Leoni. "Welcome to MBL Discount Toys. What can we get for you today?"

"I only have this," said the girl in a voice barely louder

than a whisper. Pinched between her thumb and forefinger was a dull nickel.

Max looked at Leoni, then back at the young girl. "Uh, sorry," he said. "But we're running a business here and uh . . . we don't have anything for a nickel."

If the girl looked shy before, now she looked embarrassed. "Sorry," she said before turning around and walking away from the table.

"Wait a minute," Leoni called out to the girl, who stopped and looked over her shoulder. "It just so happens that we're having a big sale today."

"What are you talking about?" said Max sharply.

"Come on, Max. You know. The big inventory clearance sale?"

"We don't have any inventory," whispered Max out of the corner of his mouth.

"Come on," Leoni pleaded. "Just this once?"

Max sighed and then looked at the girl, whose sad eyes suddenly showed a glimmer of hope. "Okay. Let me check the warehouse and see what we have in that price range."

Max ducked down behind the table and when he stood up, he was holding a gray-and-white stuffed kitten. At the sight of it, the girl's hopeful eyes looked suddenly watery.

"How did you know?" she asked softly. "That's exactly

what I wanted." She walked cautiously back to the table as if still unconvinced that this was all happening. Max handed her the kitten, and she pulled it to her chest and rubbed her cheek against its fur.

"Thank you."

"We aim to please," said Max.

The girl handed Max the nickel, but before he could take it, Leoni waved her off. "It's okay," she said. "This one comes with a five-cent manufacturer's rebate."

"A what?" said Max. Leoni responded only with a stern look. "Oh, right. I forgot about the rebate."

"Thanks," said the girl. "Merry Christmas."

"Merry Christmas," said Leoni.

She and Max continued to smile until the girl had crossed the street. Then Max's smile disappeared quite abruptly. "What was that all about?" he demanded. "The dog is six hundred bucks. How am I gonna get enough money if we keep handing out toys for free?"

"It was just once," said Leoni. "Think of it as a promotional giveaway. Just imagine all the free word-of-mouth advertising we're gonna get."

No sooner had she finished than she looked up to see the shy girl standing before them again, this time with a very stern and proper-looking woman at her side.

"My daughter has something to say to you," the woman declared.

"But, Mom," the girl whispered. "I didn't steal it. I bought it."

"You bought that with a nickel?" the girl's mother asked incredulously. "Now tell them you're sorry and give it back."

The girl sighed and reluctantly handed the kitten back to Max.

"No," said Max. "She didn't steal it, ma'am. It was part of a . . . promotional campaign."

"Promotional campaign?" the woman echoed.

"Our prices on toys are so low, it's like we're practically giving them away," said Leoni in her most convincing voice.

The woman apologized to her daughter for having doubted her, then turned to Max. "Listen," she said. "I don't suppose you have a toy pirate ship. My son's been asking for one and . . ."

Before she could finish her sentence, a hand, clutching a toy pirate ship, shot up from beneath the table. The woman gasped at the sight of it.

"This is our most popular model," said Max.

"It's perfect," said the woman as she took it from Max and examined it closely. "But I think it's probably a little over my budget. How much is it?"

"Half the price of Rainforest," said Max. "And with no shipping."

"Or handling," came a voice from under the table.

"Do you have a cell phone?" Leoni asked the woman.

"Well, of course," the woman replied, removing the phone from her pocket.

"Just look up the price on Rainforest and we'll cut that in half," said Max.

The woman tapped away at her phone, and when the web page loaded, she sighed and handed the ship back to Leoni. "Eighty-nine dollars and ninety-nine cents," she said. "So even at forty-five, it's still out of my range. But thank you very much, and best of luck to you."

"Wait," said Leoni, pushing the ship back into the woman's hands. "How about twenty?"

"Twenty?" The woman looked the ship over again. "I could do twenty."

"Sold," said Leoni.

The woman smiled and handed the ship to her daughter to hold while she fished the cash from her purse and handed it to Max.

"Thank you," said Max.

"No, thank you," said the woman. "Seriously, you have no idea what you've just done. I'm going to tell everyone I know to shop here. Merry Christmas."

"It sure is," said Leoni as the woman and her daughter turned and walked away.

Max sighed and leaned back against the table. "Well, this has been a huge waste of time."

"What?" said Leoni. "She wasn't going to buy it at forty-five, so at least we have twenty bucks. Minus my commission, of course."

"What about my commission?" said Baxter from beneath the table.

"Warehouse workers don't get commission," said Leoni. "Hey, look. More customers."

The customers to whom Leoni was referring were two cops in full uniform. One was smaller than the other, but both were considerably larger than the three kids on the other side of that rickety card table.

"Good morning, gentlemen," said Max. "What can we get for you today?"

"I'm Officer Martinez," said the shorter of the two. "And this is Officer Reynolds. I don't suppose you have a business license for this."

"Well . . . uh . . . you see . . . ," Max stammered.

"We don't need one," said Leoni.

"Excuse me?" said Officer Reynolds.

"We don't need one," Leoni restated. "You see, we're a nonprofit organization."

"Nonprofit?"

"Yes," Leoni confirmed. "One hundred percent of all proceeds will go to the, uh . . . Puppy Rescue and Adoption Fund."

"Yes," Max quickly agreed. "Also known as . . . PRAF."

"PRAF?" said Officer Martinez. He turned to his partner. "What do you think, Earl?"

Officer Reynolds nodded and stuck out his lower lip. And while Max and Leoni fully expected the next words from his mouth to be *You're under arrest*, instead he said, "Sounds like a good cause to me." Then he turned to the people walking by and said, "Listen up, folks. Get your toys right here. Help save the puppies."

A man in a suit hurried by, completely ignoring the officer until Reynolds smacked him across the shoulder. "Hey, pal. What's your problem? You got something against puppies?"

CHAPTER 15

COLD HARD CASH

If there's anything we know about reindeer, besides the fact that they can fly and have a fierce appetite for thin-crust pizza, it's that they do not appreciate anyone riding on their backs. They are also not fond of high-pitched noises like the ones that were coming out of Skhiff as the city skyline finally came into view.

"There it is," shouted Eldor to Skhiff, who sat behind him, clinging tightly to his friend's squishy midsection. "Hang on! We're going in!"

With a quick twist of the reins, Blitzen went into a steep dive, causing Skhiff to dig his fingernails into Eldor's side. "Hey!" screamed Eldor. "Easy on the love handles, brother elf."

But Skhiff refused to loosen his grip until finally Blitzen executed a four-point landing in the parking lot of a two-story motor lodge called the Budget Eight Motel. "We made it!" whooped Skhiff as he clambered off the reindeer's back. So grateful was Skhiff to be on solid ground again that he thought about kissing it, until he took a closer look at all the litter and unidentifiable stains.

Eldor instructed Blitzen to wait outside while he and Skhiff entered the small motel office, where a thin woman was chewing gum as if it owed her money.

"Can I help you?" the woman asked between loud smacks of gum. Perhaps because she had lived in the big city most of her life, the sudden appearance of two tiny men in slim tights and green stocking caps did not seem to faze her in the least.

"Yes, we need a room," said Eldor.

"For how many nights?" asked the woman flatly.

"As many as it takes."

The woman slid a registration form across the counter, and Eldor rose to his tiptoes to have a look at it. "Fill this out and sign it at the bottom," she said. "This is a nonsmoking room, and we have a strict no-pets policy."

"No problem there," Eldor replied. "We don't smoke, and we're both allergic to dogs and cats."

"And reindeer," Skhiff added, which earned him a sharp jab in the ribs from Eldor.

"And elephants," Skhiff stammered. "And all four-legged creatures. Hamsters, unicorns, moose. You name it, it makes us itchy all over. So, can we have the key now?"

At that very moment, closer to the motel than Eldor and Skhiff ever would have suspected, Max and his friends were using the red bag to make toys as if they were going out of style, which they absolutely were not. Word was out. Their toys were the cheapest anywhere, with all proceeds going to a worthy cause. As a result, people were lined up around the block. By the time the last customer of the day stepped up to the table, the money box was overflowing.

"Good afternoon, sir," said Leoni. "What can we get for you today?"

"I don't know," said the man, looking over the few items on the table. "I don't think you have what I'm looking for."

"Sure we do," said Max. "Baxter?"

With a grunt, Baxter appeared from beneath the table and hoisted up a metal ride-on fire engine complete with little wooden ladders and a brass bell. The stunned man leaned on the table as if he'd just lost his balance. "Wow," he said, running his hand across the smooth, metal surface of the toy truck. As he did, Max noticed his eyes were suddenly teary.

"I used to have one of these as a kid," sniffed the man. "I've been looking for one just like this . . . for years." Then the man narrowed his eyes and looked at Max. "But you knew that, didn't you? How? How did you know?"

Max shrugged. "Not sure, really. Just a lucky guess, I suppose."

"Lucky for me," said the man as he fished out his wallet. "How much?"

"Half the price of Rainmaker," said Max.

"They don't have these on Rainmaker," the man said. "Trust me, I've looked. Many times."

"Okay," said Leoni with a shrug. "Then how about . . . $79.99?"

"Sure," said the man, enthusiastically pulling out his wallet and removing a crisp one-hundred-dollar bill. The man handed Leoni the money, and when she offered him his change, the man said, "Keep it. You made my Christmas. My kid's gonna love this—just like I did when I was his age."

As the man lugged the heavy toy away, Leoni quickly packed up the display toys and took down the card table before any more customers could come by. Max sat on a bus stop bench and counted the money in the cashbox.

"Well?" said Baxter, standing over Max's shoulder.

"Twelve hundred and fifty-four dollars," Max announced.

"Whoa, we're millionaires," shouted Baxter, performing a victory dance that involved a lot of arm flailing.

"Well . . . not quite yet," said Max. "But we will be. All of us. And we'll all live together in a huge house. And I won't have to wash dental floss or cut toilet paper squares into smaller pieces to save money."

"And my mom won't have to work anymore," said Leoni.

"And neither will my dad," said Baxter.

"Your dad doesn't have a job," Leoni reminded Baxter.

"I know," said Baxter. "And now he can keep not having one!"

"This thing is amazing," said Max, staring at the bright-red bag resting in his lap. "And it's going to change so many lives in so many ways."

"Starting with yours," said Leoni with a smile. "Whaddaya say, Max? Shall we go get your dog?"

CHAPTER 16

TWICE THE PRICE

The owner of Jimmy O'Reilly's Pets was a man named Edward Cook. He had purchased the store twenty years ago and never bothered to change the name, probably due to the fact that Edward Cook's Pets would make it very tempting for pranksters to paint over the apostrophe on the sign.

When Max, Leoni, and Baxter walked in, Mr. Cook was sprinkling some fish food into a large aquarium. He completely ignored the three children until Leoni loudly cleared her throat.

"Can I help you?" the man replied without taking his eyes off the fish.

"You sure can," said Max, barely able to contain his excitement. "We want to buy that dog in the window."

Mr. Cook glanced down at Max, then went right back to his fish feeding. "And where are your parents?"

"Well," said Max. "I never really had a dad. And my mom died in a car accident three years ago."

Mr. Cook sighed and shook his head, then turned his back on the kids and walked toward the register. "I'm sorry to hear that, kid," he muttered over his shoulder. "But you'll have to come back with a grown-up. Or when you're eighteen."

"Eighteen?" Max spluttered. "He'll be eight years old by then."

"Yeah, that's like a hundred in dog years," Baxter explained.

Max just stood in the fish aisle, feeling as if life had dealt him yet another blow. And then it did, literally, when Leoni hit him hard in the shoulder with her elbow.

"Ow! Why'd you hit me?" Max complained.

"Here," she said, holding out her empty right palm. "Give me the money."

"What are you going to do with it?"

"I'm gonna buy a dog."

"But . . ."

"The money."

Max handed Leoni the entire wad of cash, and then he and Baxter followed her as she strode to the front of the store where Mr. Cook was busy filling a huge glass jar with dog biscuits.

"Okay, how much?" asked Leoni.

"How much for what?" replied Mr. Cook.

"The dog in the window. What's your price?"

"The dog is six hundred dollars for anyone over eighteen or in the presence of a parent or legal guardian," said Mr. Cook impatiently. "Anyone else is wasting my time."

The sound of Leoni slamming the large roll of cash onto the countertop caused Mr. Cook to flinch. "How about twelve hundred and fifty-four dollars?" said Leoni. "Cash."

Mr. Cook said nothing. He just stared at the pile of bills in front of him and, for a moment, bit his lip.

"Well?" said Leoni. "What do you say?"

"What do I say?" said the man, smiling for the first time. "I say, will you be needing a leash with that?"

CHAPTER 17

A BOY AND HIS DOG

Max rolled along the patchy grass of the vacant lot, locked in a wrestling match with Plato, the twelve-week-old Airedale terrier he'd just bought. Plato growled and tugged on the boy's jacket sleeve. Smiling so wide that his jaw ached, Max couldn't remember being this happy at any time in the past three years.

"Aaah," he yelled playfully as Plato leaped onto his chest and began nibbling at his left earlobe. "Quick! The bag," he called out to Baxter. "Look inside."

Baxter quickly picked up the red bag, then turned it upside down and gave it a few shakes until a single tennis ball dropped at his feet. "Now throw it," Max called out.

Baxter picked up the ball and skipped it across the frozen

ground. Plato tumbled off Max's chest and scrambled after the ball on clumsy puppy legs. Max took the opportunity to stand up and brush himself off.

"He sure is great, isn't he?" said Max, like a proud father watching his kid win a gold medal.

"I'm so glad you got him," Leoni agreed. "We're all gonna have lots of fun together."

"Hey, he could be our official fort mascot," said Baxter excitedly.

In the time it took Max and Leoni to agree wholeheartedly, their new official mascot had scrambled back. Panting heavily, Plato dropped a ball at Max's feet. Not the tennis ball Baxter had thrown but a partially inflated football, well scuffed and covered in duct tape.

"Hey, where'd you get this old thing?" said Max, bending over to pick up the misshapen ball.

His question would quickly be answered by a shout from across the lot as two older boys ran toward them. "Hey!" said one of them. "Your dog stole our ball."

"Sorry about that," said Max as the two boys approached. "He's just a puppy. He doesn't know any better."

"No problem," said the taller of the two boys. "He's pretty cute. For a football thief."

Max smiled and tossed the ball to the boys, but before they ran off to resume their game, Leoni stopped them.

"Wait a minute. That's your ball?"

"Yeah?" said one of the boys, not sure exactly what Leoni might be implying.

"It's pretty junky."

At first the boys looked a bit insulted, but when it came right down to it, they couldn't disagree. It was a pretty junky ball. In fact, it was barely a ball at all anymore. "Yeah," the smaller boy agreed. "But it's all we got."

"Go on, Max," said Leoni. "Give 'em a new one."

"What?" Baxter objected. "We can't be giving away free toys."

"Why not?" asked Max. "I've got my dog. We have the opportunity to change lives with this bag. And not just our own."

Baxter tried to think of a reason not to give the boys a new football and couldn't come up with a good one. "Okay," he said with a shrug. "Like you said: Why not?"

He handed the bag to Max, who reached inside and pulled out a football with bright-white laces and not a single trace of duct tape. "Here you go," he said, tossing the ball to the boys. "A little something for your trouble."

The boys examined the ball carefully, as if this whole thing might be some sort of trick. "Genuine cowhide," said the taller boy, reading directly from the ball.

"Official size and weight," confirmed the other. "And

it's signed by the NFL commissioner."

"It's almost too nice to use," said the first boy.

"Don't worry," said Max. "If it wears out, come find me. I'll give you another one."

"Seriously?"

"Sure." Max shrugged.

The boys thanked Max several times until it was almost awkward, then finally ran off to try out their new ball.

"Wow," said Max, his face locked in a broad smile. "That felt pretty good."

"Yeah." Leoni nodded in agreement. "We should do it again."

Just a few blocks away there was another lot that tried to pass itself off as a park, where younger kids hung out. It was known among the locals as Tetanus Park because of its rusted old jungle gym and swing set with one remaining swing, suspended from equally rusty chains. They decided this would be the perfect place to spread some much-needed Christmas joy. Max slung the red bag over his shoulder and then scooped up Plato, and the three of them set out on their mission.

They were only halfway to their destination when Plato suddenly whimpered at the sound of a high-pitched scream.

CHAPTER 18

THE LEGEND OF TOY MAN

A second scream echoed off the brick apartment buildings that lined the streets. Max cocked his head, trying to get a read on just where it originated. "I think it's coming from over there."

"No," said Leoni. "Look."

"Fire," said Max at the sight of the thick black smoke spiraling into the air. "Looks like it's on 27th. Let's go!"

The screams grew louder as they sprinted down 28th Avenue, then cut through an alley and rushed out onto 27th, where they found the source of both the screaming and the smoke. By the time they got to the old brick building, there were already a dozen or so adults and children standing on the sidewalk below, looking up at the young girl leaning out of the fifth-floor window.

A construction worker in a fluorescent vest tried to get the girl to stop screaming and to listen to what he was saying, which was becoming more difficult as distant sirens became louder with each passing second. "You've got to jump!" he yelled. "It's okay. I'll catch you. I promise."

"I can't!" the frightened girl yelled back, tears streaming down her face. "It's too far!"

"What wrong with her?" asked Baxter. "She has to jump."

"She's afraid," said Leoni. "It's a long way down. And what if he doesn't catch her?"

Just then a young thin woman pushed her way past them and rushed toward the building.

"Wait!" cried the construction worker, running after the desperate woman. "You can't go in there!" The worker managed to grab the woman by the arm before she could rush inside.

"That's my daughter!" she cried. "Let me go!"

The sight of the girl's mother willing to risk her life to save her child caused a lump to form in Max's throat. "No," he said. "This is not going to happen. Not today. Here," he said and thrust the dog into Leoni's arms. "I've got an idea."

Max pushed his way through the growing crowd. "Move

out of the way," he cried. "Get back!"

"Hey, get outta here kid," yelled a large man in a ball cap. "What do you think you're doing?" The man shoved Max aside and Max responded by holding the big red bag upside down. "Teddy bears!" he shouted.

As all eyes remained on the little girl, it was a few seconds before anyone noticed the wave of teddy bears, in all colors and sizes, pouring from the big red bag. The bears continued to multiply as Max ran in circles, shouting, "Pile them up! Come on, everybody, pitch in! Make a pile!"

Without hesitation, the entire crowd, including the construction worker and the little girl's mother, began tossing teddy bears until the pile became a mound and the mound became a hill, fifteen feet tall.

"Okay," Max called up to the girl. "Now you can jump. The teddy bears will catch you."

The girl looked slightly less uncertain than she had been but still said, "I can't."

"You can do it, honey!" the girl's mother shouted. "You'll be okay. I promise."

"I'll make you a deal," said Max. "If you jump into this pile of teddy bears, you can have them all." Max grabbed one of the bears from the pile. "See this one?" he

said. "He can't wait to meet you."

The girl looked at the bear's smiling face and hopeful eyes, then at her mother's desperate face. She swung one leg over the windowsill then the other until she was sitting fifty feet above the giant mound of stuffies. The crowd grew silent as the sirens grew louder. The girl closed her eyes and took a deep breath. And then she jumped.

The second she disappeared into the pile of bears a cheer rose up from the bystanders. Some of them ran toward the pile and began frantically tossing teddy bears aside until, finally, they found the girl, crying but unhurt, clutching a teddy bear in her arms.

Max stood and watched as the girl's mother wrapped her up in a tear-filled hug. Max felt some tears of his own running down his cheeks as two fire trucks screeched to a halt in front of the building and firefighters scrambled into action, shouting at people to get out of the way.

"That was awesome," said Leoni.

"Yeah," Baxter agreed. "Nice job, my friend."

Max looked away from the scene, wiped his tears off with his sleeve, and said, "Come on. We have to get out of here."

"What?" Baxter spluttered. "Are you kidding? They're about to put out a burning building."

But Max didn't wait. He took Plato from Leoni and walked at a brisk pace away from the fire and from the growing crowd.

"But why?" Leoni asked as she and Baxter hurried to catch up. "You're a hero. Don't you want to bask in the glory?"

"He's not a hero," said Baxter. "He's a superhero. He's like . . . Toy Man."

"Toy Man," Leoni echoed. "I like it."

"Hey, can I be your sidekick?" Baxter pleaded. "I could hold the bag for you when you're not using it."

"Toy Man and Bag Boy," said Leoni.

"Bag Boy?" said Baxter. "Why not Bag Man?"

"Toy Man and Bag Man?" Leoni scoffed. "That sounds dumb."

"Hey, I'm the one who's gonna be famous, so I should get to choose my own sidekick name," Baxter argued.

Now two full blocks from the scene of the fire, Max stopped and turned to face his friends. "Would you knock it off with all this famous stuff?"

"Hey, what's your problem, Toy Man?" asked Baxter.

"You don't get it," said Max. "When we sold all those toys in front of Hinkleman's, people had no idea where they came from. We just pulled them out from under the table.

Do you know what's gonna happen once everyone realizes it's the bag that makes the toys? Everyone's gonna want it."

"The government," whispered Leoni, suddenly looking around suspiciously. And then, even more quietly, "The military."

Baxter scoffed. "What the heck would the military want with a bag that makes toys?"

"If they can find out how it works, maybe they could create a bag that makes killer robots."

"Oh yeah," said Baxter, quickly jumping on board with the military angle. "Or they could build a giant bag that makes giant killer robots."

"Whatever," said Max. "The point is we should probably lie low until all this blows over. No selling toys, no giving away toys, no talking about the bag for a few days. Got it?"

"Got it, Toy Man," said Baxter.

Max just looked at his friend, smiled, and simply said, "Shut up, Bag Boy."

CHAPTER 19

THE COMPETITION

Steve Bozeman tugged at the collar of his turtleneck sweater, his face the color of raw hamburger. Sitting at his desk, he fixed his bloodshot eyes on the document resting in front of him. Standing to either side of him were his newly hired bodyguards, two very big, very mean men—just as he had requested. To his left was Lanny, a former police officer with a rectangular jaw and a military buzz cut. To his right stood Dutch, who had played offensive tackle for the Cleveland Browns before sustaining a career-ending groin injury.

By contrast, Edison, standing across from Bozeman, looked like a bamboo shoot with glasses.

"Perhaps you can explain this to me, Edison," said Bozeman, aggressively flipping through the pages of the document. "I've bought up every brick-and-mortar toy store in the entire area. And yet online orders are not up one bit, which makes no sense considering that we are now the only game in town."

"Well, actually we're not quite the only game in town, I'm afraid," said Edison.

"What do you mean?" asked Bozeman, looking up from the charts.

Edison responded by turning on the enormous flat-screen TV mounted on the far wall of the office. "I think you should see this," he said.

On the screen a news reporter was speaking into the camera as firefighters worked to put out a house fire behind her.

"When firefighters responded to this house fire in the fifteen-hundred block of 27th Avenue, they had no idea that another hero had gotten here before them," the reporter said. "With eight-year-old Kenzie Allen trapped on the fifth floor, witnesses say that a young boy, perhaps ten or twelve years old, and armed only with a large red cloth bag, produced this pile of teddy bears you see behind me, which enabled the frightened girl to jump to safety."

The scene cut suddenly to some very shaky cell phone footage of Max using the bag to create the massive mound of teddy bears.

"*Channel Seven News* has obtained these images, which appear to show what some are calling a Christmas miracle—the boy producing hundreds of teddy bears directly from the bag."

Bozeman's eyes nearly leaped from his head as he sprang to his feet and shot his index finger out in the direction of the TV. "Wait!" he shouted. "Pause that!"

Edison did as he was told, and Bozeman walked around his desk and toward the TV, squinting at it the entire way. "Back it up a little," he said.

With the remote Edison reversed the video slowly.

"A little more," said Bozeman, his scrunched-up face now just inches from the screen. "There! Stop!"

The TV showed a distant and slightly grainy view of Max's face. "That's him!" Bozeman declared, stabbing the screen with his index finger, leaving an oily smudge over Max's face. He removed his cell phone from his pocket and brought up the picture he had taken earlier. Holding the phone next to Max's frozen image on the TV, he declared, "That's the little hooligan who attacked me with the bedpan!"

"Apparently he's become something of a local hero," Edison offered. "He's been selling toys at half the price of Rainforest. If you watch the rest of the news story . . ."

"I don't need to watch the rest of the story," seethed Bozeman. "What I need is to find out who's supplying this young criminal with all these toys he's selling."

"Well," Edison persisted, "if you watch the rest of the story, you'll see that the toys seem to come from that red bag he has."

"The toys come from the bag?" scoffed Bozeman. "Sure. And the paste I used to brush my teeth this morning came from the tube. Someone is supplying him with the toys—and my money is on the Swinson brothers."

"Now listen to me, you two." Bozeman swung around and cast his eyes on Lanny and Dutch. "I want you to locate this kid so we can shut this down once and for all. Is that clear?"

"Yes, sir, Mr. Bozeman," said Lanny. "Me and Dutch will get on it right away."

"You can count on us," Dutch agreed with a smile that revealed several missing teeth.

"Good," said Bozeman. "This young man needs to learn that if you play with fire, you *might* get burned. But if you mess with Steve Bozeman, you most definitely will."

❅

Dutch and Lanny ventured out into the neighborhood to find the kid selling toys for half the price of Rainforest. They searched for three days and found no such person anywhere. They did, however, see plenty of kids playing with brand-new, expensive-looking toys.

Tired and ready to give up, the two thugs stood on the corner and watched as a boy with holes in his jacket and no laces on his shoes came whizzing toward them on a shiny new scooter, zigzagging around small patches of snow and ice. As he passed, Dutch reached out and grabbed the boy by the collar of his coat and lifted him into the air. His scooter continued on until it slammed into a dumpster and clattered to the sidewalk.

"Hey, that's my new scooter!"

"And quite a nice one at that," said Lanny. "Where'd you get the cash for it?"

"I've been saving up my tooth fairy money." The boy flashed a smile revealing several missing teeth. "Look."

"You got eighty bucks from the tooth fairy?" Dutch snarled, showing the gaps in his own mouth.

"No, I got fifty cents," said the boy. "How much did *you* get?"

"You don't get money from the tooth fairy for a punch in the mouth," said Lanny, smiling toothlessly. "Now one more time. Where'd you get the eighty bucks? Cuz that's how much those scooters cost."

"Not if you get 'em from Toy Man, they don't," the boy said. "He sells toys to kids for whatever they can afford. Sometimes he just gives them away. Could you please put me down now?"

"Just as soon as you tell us where this guy is selling his toys."

"Oh, Toy Man isn't selling toys today," the boy replied. "He closed up shop so he could play with his new puppy. But if you really need a toy right away, I'm sure he'd sell you one. I could ask him for you. He's a personal friend of mine."

"Thanks, but we'd like to ask him ourselves," said Dutch, finally lowering the boy to the ground.

"In that case," said the boy, "you might want to head over to the vacant lot on 29th. He usually hangs out there."

CHAPTER 20

BAG BOY'S BIG MOUTH

Max was right. He had been able to figure out a way to get around Mrs. Derooey's no-pets policy. With a pogo stick from the bag, he found he was able to jump high enough to grab the bottom of the fire escape and pull himself up. From there he could climb in and out of his bedroom window without having to encounter the strict apartment manager.

As for the Plimptons, the apartment was kept so dark there was a better chance of them tripping over the dog than seeing it. And any unsavory puppy smells could easily be blamed on the seldom-flushed toilet.

But after three days of lying low in the apartment, Plato

was becoming increasing restless. Max knew he had to get him outside soon. Max was therefore overjoyed when a baby panda was born at the local zoo, knocking the whole Toy Man story completely off the front pages.

Baxter and Leoni were equally happy with the news, as it meant they could finally return to the park where they could play with Plato and hand out free toys.

"Okay, okay," said Baxter to the two dozen kids who had gathered around Max. "Form a line. No pushing. Don't worry, there's enough for everyone."

"I believe you've been wanting this," said Max as he pulled a Hot Wheels racing set from the bag and handed it to a young boy, who practically fell over at the sight of it.

"How did you know?" he said with a smile so big that it looked as though his face might break.

"Beats me," said Max. He tossed the tennis ball and Plato went scampering after it. "Just popped into my head. Anyway, have fun with it."

"I will. Thanks a lot, Toy Man."

As the boy turned to leave, Max stopped him. "Wait a minute. You said Toy Man. Where did you hear that?"

"I heard it from Bag Boy," said the boy, nodding toward Baxter.

Max turned to find Baxter whistling softly and kicking at the dirt. "I thought we discussed this," he said.

"Huh? Oh yeah," said Baxter. "I guess I sort of forgot."

"You sort of forgot?"

"So I told one kid."

"It doesn't matter. Do you have any idea what could happen if . . . wait a minute. Where's Plato?"

"He's over there," said Leoni. "Look."

Across the way, Plato was jumping, panting, and twirling in front of two large men, backlit by the late afternoon sun. One of the men held the tennis ball just out of the dog's reach.

"Hey!" shouted Max. "That's my ball. Could you toss it back, please?"

But the man holding the ball did not toss it back. In fact, he ignored Max's request altogether and, instead, he squatted down and scooped Plato up into his arms.

"Let him go," Leoni yelled, leading the way as the three friends sprinted across the park.

"Hey, hey . . ." Max panted as he slowed to a jog and then stopped within arm's reach of the men. "That's my puppy."

"Lucky boy," said Lanny. "He's a cute one, all right. You want to take extra care with a dog like that, make sure nothing bad happens to him."

Lanny and Dutch laughed as Dutch petted the dog in a way that seemed less than friendly.

"I'd like him back, please," said Max, boldly stepping forward, his arms outstretched.

"Sure. You can have your dog back," said Lanny. "All you gotta do is answer a couple of questions . . . Toy Man."

Max turned and glared at Baxter. "Okay, maybe I told a couple people," Baxter admitted.

"We wanna know who you're working for," Lanny continued.

"I'm ten years old," said Max. "I don't work for anybody."

"Yeah," said Leoni. "Haven't you ever heard of child labor laws?"

Plato let out a soft whimper as Dutch squeezed him just a little tighter.

"Okay," said Baxter. "He answered your question, now give him back his dog."

"Yeah, give him back his dog," echoed the boy with the Hot Wheels set.

Dutch and Lanny looked around and noticed then that they were completely surrounded by kids, most of them holding brand-new toys.

"You boys and girls mind your own business," Lanny sneered. "This is a matter between Mr. Bozeman and little Toy Man here."

"Bozeman?" said Leoni. "The Rainforest guy?"

"That's right," said Lanny. "He's incredibly rich and

incredibly powerful. Now, one more time. Tell us who's supplying you with the toys."

"No one's supplying us," said Baxter. "We get 'em from the bag. Duh." This resulted in an elbow to the ribs and a stern look from Max.

"Shut up, would ya?"

"What do you mean, you get them from the bag?" asked Dutch. "Do we look like idiots to you?"

"No," said Leoni. "But once you start talking, that changes everything."

Like most of the kids in the crowd, Baxter found this hilarious and laughed so hard that his nose started to run. This angered Dutch to the point that he reached out and grabbed Baxter by his jacket collar. The move allowed Plato to wriggle free from Dutch's grip. The puppy tumbled to the ground and ran to Max, who quickly scooped him up.

Dutch barely noticed that his hostage had escaped. He was focused now on the ten-year-old kid who dared laugh in his gap-toothed face. "You think that's funny, you little punk?"

"Hey, leave him alone," shouted a girl holding a new leather volleyball.

"Yeah, he's our friend," said a boy with a train set tucked under his arm.

The closer the kids moved toward Dutch and Lanny,

the more uncomfortable the men became. "Hey, take it easy," Lanny chuckled nervously. "We're just here to ask a few questions, that's all."

But when Lanny turned back toward Max to ask those questions, he found that the boy with the puppy and the big red bag had disappeared.

"Hey! Where'd he go?"

"There he is," said Dutch, aiming a meaty finger toward the other end of the playground. Max, Baxter, and Leoni were running as fast as their legs would take them. "Get him!"

By the time Lanny and Dutch could push their way through the crowd of kids, Max and his friends had reached the end of the vacant lot. They zigzagged down the sidewalk, dodging the lunchtime crowd, while Lanny and Dutch were not so polite, bumping and shoving people aside.

"Look out. Outta the way," they shouted as they closed in on Max and his friends.

Max noticed a small break in the otherwise nonstop traffic. "This way," he shouted, and dashed out into the street, with Baxter and Leoni close behind. The gap closed just as Lanny and Dutch crossed after them, resulting in the honking of horns, the screeching of brakes, and the yelling of some rather inappropriate words.

Nobody knew the city quite like Max. He led his two friends down a narrow alley and into a large park, where they circled around to the far side of a large duck-filled pond, confident that they had lost the two men. But when they looked back, they found that, like zombies that just keep on coming, the thugs were still in hot pursuit.

"These guys just don't give up," said Max. He stopped running and turned toward the approaching men.

"What are you doing?" Leoni said, tugging on Max's sleeve. "Let's go."

Instead, Max looked up a steep, grassy slope to his right. "This way," he shouted. With no time to question or argue, Baxter and Leoni followed Max up the sharp incline, their legs burning as they climbed higher and higher. When they finally reached the top, Max stopped once more, further confusing his friends.

"Max, come on," Baxter pleaded.

"Just wait," said Max, watching as the two men continued running next to the pond. "Here." He handed Plato to Leoni, then took the big red bag and held it upside down.

Lanny and Dutch began scampering up the embankment, making Baxter and Leoni more nervous with every step they took. "Max," Leoni shouted.

"It's okay," said Max. "Hold. Hold." The men were now only fifteen feet below them.

"He's lost it," said Baxter to Leoni. "He's gone totally crazy."

"Hold," Max said once more, then, "Now!"

Like a very sudden, very colorful hailstorm, thousands of marbles spilled from the bag and ran down the slope straight for Lanny and Dutch.

The soles of their feet met with the cascading marbles. Fighting for traction, they found themselves slipping and sliding down the slope in an avalanche of tiny glass balls before falling into the pond with two very large splashes.

"Yes!" shouted Leoni and Baxter together.

One by one, Max high-fived his two friends, then shouted, "Let's get out of here!"

They ran off in the direction of the fort as Lanny and Dutch dragged themselves from the freezing water.

"Did you see that?" Dutch said, his remaining teeth chattering rapidly. "The chubby kid wasn't lying. That little runt really does get the toys straight from the bag."

CHAPTER 21

IN THE DOG HOUSE

The next morning, Max awoke to the sounds of whimpering and the feeling of a puppy pawing gently at his shoulder.

"Okay, okay." Max yawned. "Hold on."

Quickly, Max put on his pants and shoes, then grabbed Plato's leash and the pogo stick so they could get back in once Plato had finished his business. With the dog tucked into his coat, Max slid his bedroom window open and stepped out onto the fire escape landing.

He made the backward climb, four flights down, then dropped the remaining eight feet to the sidewalk. He removed Plato from his coat and set the dog down on the sidewalk.

"I know you don't like this," he said, attaching the leash to Plato's collar. "But it's the law. And we don't want to break the law."

"Or the rules."

Max spun around to find, standing right in front of him, Mrs. Derooey.

"Hello, young man," she hissed.

"Oh, uh . . . hi, Mrs. Derooey," Max stammered in return.

"And just what do we have here?"

Plato instantly growled at the woman, forcing Max to apologize. "Sorry about that. He's just learning. His name is . . ."

"Unimportant," the stern woman interrupted.

"What?"

"His name," she repeated. "Entirely inconsequential. It has no bearing on the fact that his presence here is in direct violation of the building's pet policy, which states that pets of any kind are strictly forbidden. This includes cats, birds, goldfish, ant farms, and especially DOGS!"

Plato growled louder, and this time Max felt even less like apologizing. "But he's just a puppy," Max reasoned. "And he's house-trained."

"Doesn't matter," said Mrs. Derooey, stepping uncom-fortably close to Max and speaking into his ear in a hoarse whisper. "If he's not gone by tomorrow, you will be. Do you understand me?"

Before Max could answer, Plato decided he was no longer able to control his bladder, though to Mrs. Derooey's horror, he was quite able to control his aim.

The resulting scream from Mrs. Derooey was so loud that it might have been heard all the way over at the Rainforest head office, if not for the fact that Steve Bozeman was far too distracted with his own problems.

"This is unacceptable!" the angry billionaire shouted.

Lanny and Dutch stood before their raging boss while Edison sat at the edge of his boss's desk taking notes, happy that, for once, the focus was not on him.

"A ten-year-old kid is stealing my business, and you two simpletons couldn't even get some basic information from him?"

"That's just a guess," said Dutch. "He could be ten and a half for all we know."

"Oh, that would explain it, then," said Bozeman, as if genuinely relieved. "You're dealing with someone of superior intellectual ability."

"It's not our fault," Lanny protested. "The kid's got that bag."

"That's right," Dutch quickly added. "He says that's where he gets all the toys he's been selling. It seems to make whatever he wants."

"Yeah," said Dutch. "Including thousands of deadly marbles."

"Marbles?"

"Yes," said Lanny. "The bag was completely empty. Then the kid turns it over and thousands of marbles come pouring out of it."

Lanny pulled a marble from his pocket and held it up to the light. "I even saved one. See? It's a cleary."

Dutch gently tossed the marble up in the air, but before it landed back in his palm, Bozeman snatched it for himself. While Dutch fully expected his new boss to hurl the marble at his head, instead he held it up to the light himself and suddenly looked far less angry and a great deal more intrigued.

"So you're saying this child actually is in possession of a magical bag that produces an infinite amount of toys?"

"I know it sounds crazy," Lanny admitted.

"Sometimes," said Bozeman, admiring his upside-down reflection on the surface of the marble, "the best ideas are the craziest ones. Tell me. What would a person have if he had a tube that produced an infinite amount of toothpaste?"

"A huge mess?" offered Dutch with a shrug.

It was at that moment that Bozeman chose to do what Dutch had originally feared he would do: Bozeman hurled the marble at his head. Luckily, Bozeman's accuracy was on par with Dutch's lack of quickness and the marble sailed far off the mark and clacked against the floor-to-ceiling office window and rolled beneath Bozeman's desk.

"No! That person would never have to buy toothpaste again!" shouted Bozeman. "And if he owned a company that sold toothpaste he'd have no overhead and he could lower his prices to the point that he could run every other toothpaste maker out of business. Now, what would happen if a person owned a toy company and came into possession of a bag that makes an unlimited amount of toys?"

"The exact same thing," said Edison.

"Yes!" said Bozeman, his eyes wild with excitement. "Now get back out there and get me that bag!"

CHAPTER 22

HOME AWAY FROM HOME

With the Plimptons sound asleep and snoring loudly in the next room, Max loaded a backpack with what few belongings he had—his clothes, a toothbrush, the red bag (of course), and the photo of him and his mother. Before he left for what he assumed would be forever, he took a look back and gently peeled the travel photos from the wall. Careful not to crinkle them, he slid them into the backpack as well.

He slung the pack onto his back and grabbed the pogo stick but quickly thought better of it. He wouldn't need it, he reasoned. After all, he would not be coming back here. Ever.

He had decided that from now on, he didn't need the Plimptons—or anyone else for that matter. From this point on, his life would be his and his alone. And it would be full of adventure, the life his mother had always wanted for him.

He took Plato in his arms, tiptoed softly through the living room, and walked out the front door without looking back.

The next morning, Baxter and Leoni met at the corner and waited for Max until they got tired of waiting. He was becoming less and less punctual since he got that bag and the dog. They decided to go to the fort without him.

The first thing they noticed when they walked in was a large pile of stuffed dogs in the middle of the living room. "I don't remember that being here yesterday," said Leoni.

"Yeah, and neither was that," said Baxter, pointing at the far wall, now decorated with photos of exotic locations from all around the world. On the LEGO end table next to the LEGO couch stood the framed photo of Max and his mother.

"Hey, guys," came a muffled and sleepy voice. The pile of dogs began to move, and a moment later, Max was crawling out on his hands and knees.

"What are you doing here?" asked Baxter. "And what's with all the stuffies?"

Max stood up and groaned like an old man stiff from the cold weather. "It's freezing here at night. And the bag doesn't make blankets."

"At night?" said Leoni. "You were here all night?"

"Yeah," said Max. "I live here now."

"You live here?" said Baxter, not certain if he heard Max correctly. "What do you mean you live here?"

"Just until I can figure things out," said Max. "The apartment manager found out about Plato and threatened to kick us all out, so I decided to just live on my own. As long as I've got the bag, I don't need anyone to take care of me. The bag gives me warmth."

Max gestured toward the stuffed dogs, then picked up a baseball bat leaning against the LEGO coffee table. "It also gives me protection."

With the bat he motioned across the room near the front door where a brand-new bike sparkled in the early morning sun. "And transportation. It even gives me food," he said as he walked into the gutted-out kitchen, where an Easy-Bake oven and a snow cone machine sat on the only remaining counter. "Everything that Plato and I need."

"Hey, where is he anyway?" asked Leoni, her eyes darting about the old house.

There was a sudden soft whimpering that appeared to be coming from somewhere under the mound of stuffed dogs.

"Not sure," said Max, walking toward the pile. "He sort of blends in. I guess I should have asked for stuffed cats, but I didn't want to freak him out."

The whimper quickly turned to a howl, and the three kids went to work, tossing stuffed dogs left and right like rescue workers after an earthquake. Finally, they unearthed Plato. The pup looked up at Max with the same hopeful eyes Max had fallen in love with on all those after-school visits to the pet store. The dog, with his tail flapping side to side, jumped into Max's arms.

"Good boy, Plato," Max said while turning his head side to side, trying to avoid being licked right on the mouth.

"So you're just gonna live here until what?" asked Leoni. "Until they tear it down?"

"No one's gonna tear this place down," said Max, having already thought this through. "Cuz I'm gonna buy it first. Then I'm gonna fix it up so we can all live here together. And all the kids in the neighborhood with nothing to do can come over and play any time they want."

"Yeah, but don't houses cost a lot of money?" asked Baxter. "Even this dump?"

"Yup," Max agreed. "Which means we're gonna have to sell a lot of toys."

With that, he grabbed the folded-up card table and walked out of the house with Leoni, Baxter, and Plato following dutifully behind.

CHAPTER 23

FINDERS KEEPERS

Two full days of traipsing aimlessly through the city had left the elves exhausted and desperate. Though to be honest, Skhiff was far more desperate than Eldor, who found that thin-crust pizza from Corsoni's could really calm the nerves.

"Okay," said Skhiff, trying his best not to lose his patience. "I'm not exactly clear on how doing this is going to help us find the bag."

"We're retracing our steps," said Eldor, who seemed entirely unfamiliar with the rules regarding talking with your mouth full. "Let's see, after we got the pizza last time, as I recall, we went to that bar down the street."

"Yeah, and got thrown out on our cans."

"Two pieces of ID," Eldor scoffed. "Seriously? I'm 209 years old."

"And this city is huge," said Skhiff. "We couldn't have lost the bag in Topeka, Kansas?"

"Yeah, it's too bad I didn't have a craving for corn dogs and deep-fried butter," said Eldor just as Skhiff stepped on a toy bulldozer and tumbled to the ground.

"Ouch! What the . . . ? Irresponsible toy owners," Skhiff groused. "Somebody could get seriously hurt."

"Oh, don't be such a ninny," said Eldor, a split second before a Frisbee hit him squarely in the forehead. "Ow! Did you see that? I am gonna sue somebody, man. You just watch me."

Skhiff looked at the Frisbee lying at Eldor's feet. He bent down and picked it up. "Hey, look at this," he said, handing the toy to Eldor.

Eldor inspected the flying disc to find it stamped with the letters *NP*. "North Pole," he gasped. "It's one of ours. We're close. I can feel it in my bones."

Just then another Frisbee flew in and hit him right between the legs. "Aaah! In the crotch? Seriously?"

As Eldor writhed in pain, Skhiff looked off to his left and rubbed his eyes in disbelief. "You're right," he said. "We are close. In fact, it would be hard to get much closer."

Eldor managed to stand up straight and look up the

street, where MBL Discount Toys was in full operation, with a long line snaking down the block and around the corner. Skhiff watched, slack-jawed, as Max pulled toy after toy from the bag.

"I don't get it," he said. "The bag is only supposed to work for Santa—and that kid's got it going like the old man himself."

"Low batteries?"

"The bag doesn't run on batteries. It runs on magic."

"Low magic, then?" said Eldor, finally able to stand up straight.

"Who cares?" said Skhiff. "Let's just get the bag and get outta here."

"Okay, and how should we go about that, do you think?" asked Skhiff as he and Eldor began walking toward the makeshift toy store.

"Don't worry," said Eldor, which had no effect whatsoever on Skhiff's worry level. "As always, Eldor has a plan."

Neither Max nor his friends noticed the two elves as they approached the table. They were too busy serving their many customers, like the boy with short hair and glasses who stepped up holding a twenty-dollar bill.

"A chemistry set?" the boy asked hopefully.

"Sure thing," said Max. He reached under the table

and the warehouse supervisor handed him a chemistry set, which Max presented to the overjoyed young scientist. The boy handed the money to Leoni.

"That's okay," she said, handing the bill back to the boy. "It's on the house."

"What?" said Max sternly. "No, no. No more free stuff."

"Not for everybody," said Leoni. "Just for kids."

"Yeah," said Baxter from beneath the table. "Kids shouldn't have to pay for toys. Only big people."

"Yeah, well, I've got mouths to feed here," said Max, nodding at Plato, who was busy gnawing on a squeaky rubber chew toy. "I've got responsibilities. I've got my future to think about."

Leoni rolled her eyes. "You sound like my mom."

"Yeah," Baxter agreed. "You sound like her mom."

"Come on, Max," Leoni whispered while the boy just stood there, caught in the middle of the argument. "That's Eugene Dooley. He goes to school with my cousin. Kid's a genius. They skipped him ahead two whole grades. He could cure cancer someday."

Max thought for a moment, then snatched the twenty from Leoni and handed the boy a ten from the change box. "Ten bucks," he said. "It's the best I can do."

"Ah man, that's harsh," said Baxter in his most disgusted tone.

Eugene Dooley, on the other hand, could not have been happier. "Thanks." He beamed, and ran off with the chemistry set under his arm. As he did, there arose a grumbling among the customers. Two funny-looking kids in green stocking caps had cut to the front of the line.

"Hey, little boys," said Leoni. "I'm afraid you'll have to wait in line just like everyone else."

"Little boys?" said Eldor to Skhiff. "The lack of respect for their elders is unbelievable."

Upon hearing Eldor's deep voice, Leoni realized her mistake. These weren't little boys at all. "Oh, sorry," she said. "I thought you were . . ."

"Little late for apologies," said Eldor. "But don't sweat it. We didn't come here to make friends. We just want our bag back. *That* bag."

"What?" said Max. "This isn't your bag."

"Technically, you're right," said Skhiff. "It's not our bag. It belongs to our boss, but we're responsible for it, so . . ."

"Yeah?" said Max. "Well, you can go back and tell that Bozeman guy to give up, cuz he's never gonna get this bag."

"Bozeman?" said Eldor, turning to Skhiff. "Have you ever heard him called Bozeman?"

"No," said Skhiff. "Clausman, maybe?"

By now Baxter had climbed out from under the table just in case any additional muscle might be needed. "Listen," he said. "If you clowns think we're going to give you this bag, you're crazy. Now leave us alone."

"Clowns?" said Eldor. "Seriously?"

Leoni leaned closer to Max. "You know, I think maybe we should close up shop for the day."

Max agreed, and his announcement to those kids still waiting in line was met with groans and pleas to stay open just a little while longer. "Don't worry," said Max. "We'll be back again tomorrow."

Max swept the building blocks off the table and into the bag. Baxter folded the card table and Leoni picked Plato up. The remaining customers shouted insults at Eldor and Skhiff, who watched helplessly as Max walked away with the bag.

"So that was your plan?" said Skhiff angrily.

"That was plan A, yes," said Eldor.

"Okay. And what's plan B?"

"I think we gotta tell 'em," said Eldor.

"No. Absolutely not," said Skhiff. "That is rule number one and you know it."

"Okay, fine," Eldor replied as Max and his friends disappeared around the corner. "Then I guess we go with plan C."

"Which is?"

"I'll hit 'em low, and you hit 'em even lower."

"What?" gasped Skhiff. "They're children."

"Children heal up fast," Eldor countered. "Besides, do you have a plan C that doesn't involve getting eaten by polar bears?"

Skhiff sighed. "Okay," he relented. "Let's do it."

Baxter was the first to hear the huffing and puffing and the pattering of elf-size feet on the pavement. "Look out!" he cried when he spun around and saw the two elves racing toward them.

Quickly, Max thought of a die-cast toy tractor and swung the suddenly heavy bag at the attacking elves. The tractor caught Eldor on the side of the head, and he immediately crumpled to the sidewalk in pain. Skhiff, on the other hand, grabbed hold of the bag as it swung past him. He held on tightly while Max spun in circles, dragging the elf across the ground, then swinging him, round and round, in the air.

"Hey, come on, kid," Skhiff pleaded. "Give it up! Please. I'm . . . starting to black out!"

But before Skhiff could black out from the g-forces, he was knocked out when he collided with a mailbox. He crumpled to the ground a few feet from his semiconscious buddy.

"Come on," said Leoni. "To the fort!"

It was only a few blocks away, but by the time the fort came into view, Max's legs were like rubber. He crawled through the hole in the fence and in through the window to the fort with Baxter and Leoni right behind.

"Wow, that was close," gasped Leoni, peering up over the window ledge.

"What do you think's going on?" Max wondered. "I mean, first that Bozeman dude sends a couple of huge guys to get the bag, then he sends a couple of tiny guys."

"Yeah," said Baxter, joining Leoni at the window. "I guess now we should be on the lookout for a couple of medium-size guys."

"That might be the dumbest thought ever expressed with words," said Leoni.

"Well, what if they find us here?" asked Baxter. "What do we do then?"

"What do we do?" Max repeated. "We fight back, that's what we do."

"With what?" asked Baxter.

"With everything we've got. It's time to initiate Operation Booby Trap."

CHAPTER 24

ELF ATTACK

With three sets of child-size footprints in the snow to guide them, it wasn't long before Eldor and Skhiff arrived at the fort.

"Looks like this is the end of the line," said Eldor, looking at the prints that led through the hole in the fence and across the yard of the old house. "Follow me."

The two elves easily climbed through the fence and crept slowly toward the house. As they did, Skhiff glanced up and was certain he saw movement through the second-story window. "It's them. They're up there."

"Okay, kids!" Eldor yelled through his tiny hands cupped around his tiny mouth. "Listen up and listen good! We've got the place surrounded! All you have to do is throw the bag out the window, and nobody gets hurt!"

Just then, the elves heard a noise above. "Look," whispered Skhiff.

It was the bag, in all its red-and-white glory, inching out the second-floor window. "Ha!" said Eldor, rubbing his palms together with glee. "See how easy that was?"

Before Skhiff could express his agreement, toys by the hundreds began spilling from the bag. Eldor and Skhiff scrambled out of the way, but not fast enough to avoid the sudden shower of countless cars, boats, trains, nine baseball bats, eight hobby horses, fourteen tricycles, and one large wooden easel.

When the cascade finally ended, there was no movement from beneath the pile for several minutes. There was only a low, painful groan, then Skhiff said, "What was that part about nobody getting hurt?"

Eldor threw a tricycle aside and sat up. A moment later, his friend managed to sit up next to him.

"All right, that's it," said Eldor. He tossed the easel away and stood up defiantly. "No more Mr. Nice Elves. I'll take the main floor. You attack from above."

"Okay," said Skhiff, too weak to argue. "I'll climb that trellis over there."

"Climb? Just upshoot," said Eldor.

"No," Skhiff replied. "You know the rules. We can't do

it in front of humans. That would break the Oath of Elves. Not gonna do it."

Eldor sighed heavily. "You and your stupid integrity."

"It's not stupid," Skhiff snapped. "If you had any integrity at all, we wouldn't be in this mess. Now if you'll excuse me, I'm going to climb up to the second floor and get that bag back and save Christmas."

Eldor watched as his friend tested the trellis for sturdiness before climbing slowly toward the second-floor window. He made it nearly to the top before the rickety wooden structure began to pull away from the house. Desperately, he reached out for something to hold on to.

In a second, there was Max, sticking his head out the window. "Pull my finger," he said.

But instead of his finger, what Max offered was a small rope with a ring at the end that Skhiff was only too happy to grab onto. When Skhiff pulled the rope, he instantly realized that he was actually holding on to the cord of an automatic inflatable raft. The rapid expansion of the raft catapulted him from the trellis, across the yard, and through the roof of an old doghouse.

In a panic, Eldor ran to the doghouse. He peered through the door to find his friend lying on his side.

"Skhiff? Are you okay?"

"Define *okay*," moaned Skhiff.

"Don't worry," said Eldor. "I promise that I will avenge your death."

"I'm not dead," Skhiff reminded Eldor.

"Of course not," said Eldor. "But just in case." He then looked back at the house and gritted his teeth in anger. How dare they treat his friend like this. Eldor skulked toward the front door and prepared to break it down. But when he gave a quick shove with his shoulder, he found that it was unlocked. He burst into the room, prepared for the worst, but found it unoccupied.

"All right, you three little piggies," he shouted. "It's all over now, cuz the big bad wolf is in the house!"

The second he had finished his declaration and before he could fully close his lips, a stream of dirty, foul-tasting water hit him in the mouth and soaked his face and shirt. He spat out the brackish water and wiped it from his eyes. He looked up to see Baxter, standing at the top of the stairs, armed with a Super Soaker.

"That's for eating Little Red Riding Hood's grand-mother," he said.

More determined than ever, Eldor let out a growl like an injured badger and raced up the stairs toward Baxter, who, inexplicably, did not run away. Instead he just stood there with an empty Super Soaker in his hand and a stupid grin on his face. When Eldor was nearly within grabbing distance, Baxter reached over and casually opened a closet at the top of the stairs releasing somewhere in the neighborhood of two thousand golf balls, basketballs, baseballs, softballs, medicine balls, and bocce balls.

Eldor tumbled downward, one painful stair at a time, until he was lying on his back on the living room floor. He sat up just in time for a late-arriving cricket ball to bounce off the bottom stair and strike him right on the tip of his nose.

"Okay, that really hurt," he said, feeling for blood.

"It did look painful," said Leoni from the landing. "You might want to put something on that." She raised a bright-orange toy gun and fired a dart, its plastic suction cup finding the exact middle of Eldor's forehead. "Sorry, missed. My mistake."

With a pop, Eldor pulled the dart from his forehead and stood up. "Okay, now I'm really mad. An extra-special kind of mad. The kind of mad that you don't want to be any part of."

As he charged toward the staircase again, Max appeared on the landing, holding the very full-looking bag. With Plato at his side, yapping angrily at the elf, Max tipped the bag toward Eldor and out came an enormous wooden dollhouse. Eldor quickly reversed course as the dollhouse tumbled toward him.

He practically flew out the door, only to find himself on the front porch in a minefield of Slinkys, the wire coils becoming wrapped around his ankles. He stumbled into a row of skateboards, strategically placed as part of Operation Booby Trap. He tried his best to maintain his balance, but that became impossible when the skateboard he'd stepped on started down the front stairs. Eldor hit the steps and was launched into an icy puddle near the old doghouse.

He crawled from the puddle just as Skhiff emerged from the doghouse. "Hey," said Eldor. "You're still alive!"

"Just barely," groaned Skhiff. "Level with me. How bad is it?"

"How bad is it?" said Eldor. "It's horrible. We're getting our butts kicked by a bunch of little kids with some toys."

"Yeah," Skhiff agreed. "It doesn't look good on paper, does it?"

"Well, this is where it all changes," said Eldor, summoning a deep-seated anger. "One final offensive that will turn the tide of the war. They may have us outnumbered, but we've got one thing they didn't count on. Courage under fire."

"Let's do it!" said Skhiff, whose war cry was soon drowned out by a loud buzzing sound coming from a squadron of several dozen remote-control fighter planes heading directly toward them.

"Stand your ground!" Eldor ordered as Max, now dressed in a World War II bomber jacket and goggles, launched plane after plane from the second-story balcony. "Never surrender! We must fight to the death!" Skhiff grabbed a rusty garbage pail lid and successfully deflected several planes before another flew in from an angle and collided with his left temple.

"Retreat!" yelled Eldor, contradicting his previous orders. Max and his friends watched and cheered as the elves scampered through the hole in the fence and took cover behind a mail truck parked on the street.

"I've said it before and I'll say it again," Skhiff panted. "Toys today are way too dangerous."

"Well, at least we're safe for now," said Eldor just as the mail truck pulled away from the curb, fully exposing them to the heavily armed kids on the balcony.

"Don't shoot! Cease fire! We give up!" shouted Eldor and Skhiff, their hands raised high above their heads.

"Why don't you guys go pick on someone your own size!" shouted Leoni.

"Yeah, I think there's a day care down the street," said Baxter.

"Oh, I get it," said Eldor, lowering his hands and planting them on his hips. "A short joke. Nice. Well, you just added insult to injury, my friend. And that's a deadly combination."

Eldor took an aggressive step toward the house, but Skhiff grabbed him by the arm and pulled him back. "Take

it easy. We just surrendered, remember?"

"Oh yeah."

"You know," said Skhiff. "I think it's time to go back to plan B."

"You mean, break rule number one?" said Eldor, not sure if he had heard his friend correctly.

"That's exactly what I mean," said Skhiff.

"Okay," said Eldor. "I hope you know what you're doing." He then cupped his hands around his mouth and yelled, "Hey, kids! Listen! We don't want any trouble, we just want to talk."

"Then start yappin'," said Baxter.

"Not here," said Eldor. "What we have to say is top secret information. We need to discuss it in private."

Both Leoni's and Baxter's first instinct was to tell the two little men exactly where to shove their suggestion. But they turned to Max. After all, he was the superhero here. "Well, Toy Man?" said Leoni. "What do you think?"

"I think we should listen to what they have to say," Max replied.

"But it could be a trap," said Baxter.

"Exactly," said Max. "That's why we need to take every precaution. And I do mean *every* precaution."

CHAPTER 25

PLAN B

Eldor and Skhiff stood in the middle of the living room, shivering. They were shivering because they were wearing nothing but their stocking caps and their official North Pole long johns. They watched as Baxter and Leoni rifled through their pants pockets, looking for weapons or anything else the elves might use to their advantage.

"Okay, I think I'm getting frostbite on my extremities," said Eldor, his teeth chattering. "And I like my extremities. They're some of my favorite parts."

"Then you'd better talk fast," said Max. "Or I'll sic my dog on you."

It may have seemed an empty threat, though Max had

no way of knowing that elves are actually quite afraid of dogs, even one so small as Plato.

"No, not the dog," pleaded Eldor. "We just need to talk to you about the bag."

"Yeah, it's like I told you . . . ," said Max.

"It belongs to Santa Claus," Skhiff interrupted, officially breaking the Oath of Elves.

"Santa Claus?" Max scoffed. "That's your top secret information? You gotta be kidding me."

"Oh, come on," said Eldor. "Seriously, I mean look at it, dude. It's big; it's red. Toys come out of it. *Hello?* Pretty obvious, I would think."

"Yeah, nice try," said Baxter. "And I suppose you two are pointy-eared elves from the North Pole."

Eldor shook his head in disappointment. "Kids today," he said to Skhiff. "So cynical." With one hand he grabbed his stocking cap, and with the other he grabbed Skhiff's and simultaneously yanked the hats away.

Leoni gasped at the sight of the pointy ears, and Baxter grimaced at the sight of Eldor's mangled one.

"Wow," said Leoni. "They really are elves."

Not nearly as impressed, Max casually pulled a pair of Spock novelty ears from the bag and placed one on each side of his head. "Hey, look everybody. I'm an elf, too."

"Yeah, but ours are real," said Eldor.

Baxter stepped toward the elves for a closer look. He reached out and gave Skhiff's left ear a sharp flick. "Ouch!" Skhiff cried.

"He's right," Baxter confirmed. "They're real."

"You think that's something," said Eldor as he walked over to the fireplace. "Check this out."

Max and the others watched as Eldor stepped inside the fireplace, then took a deep breath and held it.

"Wow, so you can hold your breath," said Max. "Very impressive."

Just like that, Eldor shot up out of sight. Baxter and Leoni were so amazed they practically fell over.

"Whoa!" said Baxter. "Did you see that?"

"I saw it, but I'm not sure I believe it," said Leoni, just as Eldor floated back down to the fireplace.

"Okay, so now what do you say?" smiled Eldor, wiping a bit of black soot from his once-white underwear as he strode confidently from the fireplace.

"It's a trick," said Max, slowly backing toward the door. "They'd do anything to get their hands on a bag that makes toys."

"What?" said Skhiff. "No, no. The bag doesn't make toys. We elves make the toys. The bag is just a transport device."

"A what?" said Leoni.

"Santa can't possibly carry enough toys in his sleigh for every child in the world," Skhiff explained. "So he uses the bag to transport them directly from the warehouse at the North Pole."

"So that's how he does it," said Baxter.

"That's right," said Eldor. "And if we don't get that bag back to Santa by tomorrow, there'll be no Christmas."

"No Christmas?" gasped Baxter.

"No Christmas, no Yuletide, no Feliz Navidad, and no Noel," said Eldor. "Not this year, not any year."

"Okay, Max, give 'em back their bag," Leoni demanded.

"No. No way," said Max. "I found it, and I'm keeping it. That's how it works."

"You can't ruin Christmas for everyone in the whole world," said Baxter. "It wouldn't be fair."

"If life were fair, I'd still have my mom," Max snapped back. "Without this bag, I'll have to go back and live with the Plimptons. And I'll have to get rid of Plato."

As Max and Baxter argued about the bag, Eldor inched toward it. Finally, he was close enough to reach out and snatch it from Max's hands.

"Aha! Got it," he said, backing away. "I'm lightning quick."

The look on Max's face was one of pure rage. So intense was it that it scared Skhiff. "Okay, easy now," he said, backing away. "Don't try to stop us. We elves have magical powers you can't even begin to comprehend."

"Yeah, well I've got some powers of my own," said Max.

Suddenly, the bag dropped to the floor with a *thud*.

"What's the matter?" asked Max, walking slowly toward the elves. "Bag getting a little heavy?"

Even pulling it together, Skhiff and Eldor struggled to drag the bag out the door. Completely full of bowling balls, some rolled out of the bag, nearly crushing the elves' tiny toes.

"How many bowling balls do we have at the North Pole?" Eldor asked his friend.

"About a hundred less than we used to have," grunted Skhiff.

Those hundred bowling balls, much too heavy for the elves to drag, were also much too heavy for the floorboards of the old house. With a sharp crack, the floor gave way and Max watched in shock as the elves, along with most of the bowling balls, disappeared into the basement below.

Baxter and Leoni rushed over to the newly made hole in the floor and peered over the edge to see the elves lying motionless, flat on their backs, surrounded by and partially covered in bowling balls.

"Are you okay?" Baxter called down.

"Nothing that a simple spine transplant won't fix," said Eldor weakly.

The now-empty bag hung from a broken board, and Max easily snatched it back.

"Come on, Max, give them the bag," Leoni pleaded.

Max found he couldn't look directly at his friends. "I'm sorry," he whispered. "I can't."

And with that, he scooped up Plato, threw the bag over his shoulder, hurried out the door, and dashed across the front yard and through the fence.

He ran only half a block before he took cover behind a dumpster, where he could secretly keep an eye on the fort. Twenty minutes later, when Baxter, Leoni, and the so-called elves finally left the house, he sneaked back in.

"I'm sorry, Plato," he said as he tiptoed toward the LEGO nightstand. "I know this is your home, too. But we can't stay here anymore. As long as we've got this bag, we're not safe. We've gotta find a new place to live. I just need to get something."

From the nightstand, Max picked up the framed photo of him and his mother. He gazed at her smiling face for a good long while, and then he spoke to the photo.

"I don't know. I don't know, Mom. Tell me. What should I do? What would you do?"

CHAPTER 26

BAG NAPPERS

A warm overnight wind had melted enough of the snow that it was finally possible for Baxter and Leoni to test out the new bikes Max had given them. Baxter struggled to keep up with Leoni as she zigzagged around potholes and mounds of dirty slush.

"Hey, wait up!" she heard from behind. But it wasn't Baxter's voice. When she looked over her shoulder, she saw Max riding toward them. She skidded to a stop and Baxter pulled up alongside her as Max approached, the red bag draped across his shoulders and flying in the breeze like a superhero's cape.

"I'm glad I found you," he said as he coasted to a stop. "I need your help."

"Let me guess," said Baxter. "You're off to steal eggs from the Easter bunny."

"Hey, maybe after that, we could roll the tooth fairy for quarters," said Leoni.

"Very funny. Come on, guys, this is serious."

Baxter was the first to notice that something was missing here. "Hey," he said. "Where's Plato?"

Max took a deep breath and looked away. When he turned back, Baxter and Leoni noticed his eyes were glossy.

"I took him back to the store," said Max, choking out the words. "Someone will give him a good home."

"You took your dog back?" gasped Leoni. "Why?"

"I moved back in with the Plimptons," Max explained. "I can't make it alone without the bag. And it doesn't belong to me. It belongs to . . . everybody. To the whole world. So let's go find those elves before it's too late."

Baxter draped his arm around Max's slumping shoulders. "You're doing the right thing," he said with a slow pat on the back.

"Yeah," Leoni agreed, and gave him a big hug. "I'm sorry you had to give Plato back. But that was a pretty awesome thing you did. Giving up your dog to save Christmas."

"I don't wanna talk about it," said Max. "Let's just go."

"They said they were staying at the Budget Eight Motel

by the bus depot," said Baxter. "Room 114."

They had only gotten a block or so when they heard the sudden revving of a car engine followed by the squealing of tires. Looking over their shoulders they saw a shiny black sedan racing up from behind.

"Look out!" cried Max.

"It's okay," said Leoni. "Don't panic."

But Baxter did the exact opposite of not panicking. He immediately lost control of his bike and swerved into Leoni's path. The resulting collision sent Baxter to the pavement and Leoni soaring over her handlebars and into a hedge.

Leoni's bike bounced off the curb and slid into Max's path. As Max went sprawling and tumbling over the two bikes on his way to the ground, the bag flew from his hands.

The black sedan lurched to a stop only a few feet away. The front passenger door flew open and out stepped Dutch. Max and his friends watched helplessly as Dutch reached down and snatched the bag from the ground.

"Pleasure doing business with you kids," he said with a snarly smile. "Oh, and, uh, merry Christmas."

With that he jumped back into the car, and it sped off.

Twelve blocks away, in Room 114 at the Budget Eight Motel, Eldor and Skhiff didn't even try to stop Blitzen from chewing on the mattress. They were far too depressed to care about such matters.

"Four hours till launch," said Eldor. He took a swig from a carton of eggnog, then passed it to Skhiff, sitting on the bed next to him. "I can't believe it, man. I can't believe you ruined Christmas for the entire world."

"Me?" Skhiff objected. "You're the one who decided to take the sleigh for a joyride."

"And you're the one who decided not to try to stop me," Eldor countered.

"What?" Skhiff spluttered. "Do you hear yourself? A sociopath is what you are."

"Name-calling is never okay."

Skhiff sighed and took a swig from the carton. "Sorry," he said.

"Ah, don't sweat it," said Eldor. "I still love you like a brother from another elfin mother. And that's not just the expired eggnog talkin'."

Skhiff pulled the carton from his lips and looked at it. "Expired?"

Suddenly there was a pounding at the door, but the elves were so depressed that it resulted in almost no discernible reaction other than Eldor managing a very disinterested, "Yeah? Who is it?"

"It's me," came the voice from the other side of the door. "Max. The kid with the bag."

Instantly their moods were transformed. Eldor and Skhiff leaped from the bed, hurried to the door, and pulled it open. Only to find three kids and no red bag.

"Whoa," said Leoni, peering past the disappointed elves. "Is that a reindeer?"

"Yup," said Eldor, watching as Blitzen filled his belly with mattress foam.

"Reindeer are totally cool," said Baxter, while the elves were thinking that reindeer were quite the opposite of that.

"Yeah, and from what I understand," said Eldor, "they're an excellent source of vitamin B12."

Blitzen stopped chewing just long enough to spit a mouthful of foam at Eldor.

"So, what's the deal?" asked Skhiff. "I thought you said you had the bag. Where is it?"

"Well, we don't exactly 'have' it," said Max, making use of air quotes. "But we know who does."

CHAPTER 27

WHERE'S THE MAGIC?

The bag lay on the floor of Bozeman's sixth-floor office, and he paced around it, yelling at it. "Make toys!" he commanded. "Now! Come on, you worthless piece of cloth. I order you to MAKE TOYS!"

Lanny and Dutch watched in silence, hoping that Bozeman's displeasure would remain focused on the bag and not turn to them.

"A dolly. A squirt gun. A lousy yo-yo. Anything!" Bozeman snarled and gave the bag a kick. He picked it up and peered inside. "Still nothing. If a little kid can work this thing, then why can't I? Are you sure you got the right bag?"

"It's definitely the right one," Dutch confirmed.

"Hey, maybe there's some kind of magic word or something," Lanny offered. "Like *shazam* or *open sesame*!"

"Try *abracadabra*," Dutch suggested. "That's a good one."

"That's ridiculous," snapped Bozeman. But a mere couple of seconds later he was shaking the bag and yelling "Shazam, open sesame, abracadabra!"

When he reached into the bag and found it still empty, he hurled it across the room.

And while Bozeman was frantically trying to figure out how the bag worked, six floors below, crouching behind a parked car, Max, Leoni, Baxter, and the elves were working on a plan to get it back.

"There's just no way," Baxter concluded. "There's no way we could break into the building, get past security, go all the way to the sixth floor, grab the bag, and get away."

"Hey, wait a minute," said Leoni to Eldor and Skhiff. "What about you guys? Didn't you say elves have magical powers we couldn't begin to comprehend?"

"Depends on what you mean by magical," said Skhiff.

"Yeah, and what you mean by *have*," added Eldor.

"What about the chimney thing?" said Max. "You could just float up there and get it."

"Are you kidding?" said Eldor. "We're built for chimneys.

That's a six-story building. We can't hold our breath that long. We'd get halfway up before we'd have to breathe and then, boom. Down we'd go. You ever drop a watermelon off a building? It'd be just like that but without all the seeds."

"So it'd be like dropping a seedless watermelon off a building?" said Leoni.

"That's right," said Skhiff with resignation. "No, I'm afraid our only marketable skill is shoveling reindeer poop."

Just then something happened to Baxter that he could never remember happening before. An idea popped into his head. And a good idea at that. "Hey," he said. "That's it: the reindeer can do it."

"Sadly, no," said Eldor. "If they could shovel their own poop, our lives would be a lot easier."

"No," Baxter said, getting more and more excited by the second. "What I mean is they can fly, right?"

Eldor looked at Skhiff, and Skhiff looked at Eldor. The two elves smiled from pointy ear to pointy ear. They high-fived each other, then gave Baxter a congratulatory smack on the back.

"You, my good man," said Eldor, "are a . . ."

"Genius?" Baxter offered.

"Hmm. No, I'm not gettin' that vibe at all," said Eldor. "But that is a pretty good idea. Now stand back while I summon that four-legged garbage disposal with a sound so high, it can only be heard by reindeer."

Eldor placed his fingers in his mouth, bit down, and blew, causing dozens of neighborhood dogs to start barking.

"Hmm," he said. "Okay, not quite high enough."

"Let me try," said Skhiff. He placed his finger and thumb in his mouth, bit down, and blew.

Two miles away, the manager of the Budget Eight Motel was sweeping the sidewalk when Blitzen's powerful hind legs blasted the door to Room 114 off its hinges, sending it sliding across the parking lot. The manager's broom fell from her hands when the next thing she saw was a reindeer walk out of the room and then bound off into the sky.

CHAPTER 28

UP ON THE ROOFTOP

"Where is that flying coatrack?" Eldor grumbled. "He should be here by now." Suddenly, Eldor felt a nudge and turned to see Blitzen standing only inches away. "Aaah!" he screamed in surprise. "Okay, that is unacceptable. Sneaking up on an elf like that."

Baxter and the others couldn't help but laugh. "Oh man," said Baxter. "I thought you were gonna pee your pants."

"Yeah, but I didn't," said Eldor. "Not even a little bit. Now listen up. This could save your life. Old Blitzen here is not exactly the jolliest of reindeer, so you all wait here while Skhiff and I ride him up to the rooftop, crawl down to the sixth floor through the air duct, and grab the bag."

But when Eldor attempted to climb aboard the reindeer, Blitzen threw a hip check and knocked the elf into a nearby lamppost.

"Whoa, whoa. Easy there," said Skhiff, walking slowly toward Blitzen.

Blitzen snorted and lowered his antlers. Skhiff froze and closed his eyes tightly as Blitzen charged toward him, then past him, right toward Max.

"Run!" yelled Leoni.

But it was too late. There was no time. All Max could do was stand his ground and pray it didn't hurt to be impaled by a set of pointy antlers. But there would be no impaling today. Instead, Blitzen skidded to a halt right in front of Max and licked Max's cheek.

Max laughed and wiped away the slobber with his jacket sleeve as Blitzen nuzzled Max with his nose.

"Hey, I think he likes you," said Baxter.

"I don't get it," said Eldor. "He hates everybody but Santa."

Blitzen suddenly lowered his head, poked his nose between Max's legs, and then threw his head back, launching Max into the air where he did a complete flip before landing on Blitzen's back in a seated position.

"Whoa, easy now," said Max, a bit dizzy from the flip.

"Hey, kid," said Eldor. "You'd better get down from there before you get hurt."

Max was thinking the exact same thing, but before he could dismount, Blitzen took off into the air. Max grabbed an antler with each hand as Blitzen flew higher and higher, Max's friends below getting smaller and smaller.

"Hey, look at me!" Max yelled down once he decided he wasn't in danger. "I'm flying!"

"Well, how do you like that?" said Eldor, with a disgusted shake of his head. "First he steals our bag, now he's jackin' our ride."

"Go, Max!" yelled Leoni.

Blitzen flew upward in a careful spiral around the building until Max could see Bozeman in the window of his sixth-floor office, still yelling at and kicking the bag. Blitzen continued up another story to the rooftop, where he made a perfectly smooth and remarkably gentle landing.

"Good boy, Blitzen," said Max. He gave the reindeer a pat on the neck and then climbed down from his mount. As he walked toward a large aluminum exhaust vent, he could hear the muffled tirade going on in the office below.

"Okay," said Max. "Wish me luck."

Slowly, he crawled through the opening of the vent, and

as he did, he could now clearly hear Bozeman yelling at the bag.

"That's it!" howled Bozeman, stomping on the bag as if it had made a nasty remark about his mother. "I'm finished with you, you worthless rag." Then he turned to Lanny. "Get me some gasoline."

"You think that's the trouble?" asked Dutch. "You think maybe the bag is out of gas?"

"No, mush head," snapped Bozeman. "If I can't use this magic bag, I'm going to make sure that nobody else can. I'm going to burn it to ashes."

Max's gasp echoed through the heating duct almost loud enough that it could be heard over Bozeman's growling.

As Lanny hurried off to find a can of gasoline, Max crept slowly through the dark vent. It was so dark, in fact, that he failed to see the drop-off until it was too late and he fell through the grating and crashed to the floor of Bozeman's office.

"What the—" shouted Bozeman.

"It's him, boss," said Dutch. He reached down with a meaty hand and picked up Max by his jacket collar. "The kid who knows how the bag works."

"Well," said Bozeman, his voice instantly softening. "If it isn't the bedpan assassin. What a delightful coincidence."

"It's no coincidence," said Max. "That's my bag, and I came to get it back."

As Max dangled in midair, Bozeman moved close enough to pinch Max's chin between his thumb and forefinger. "Listen to me, junior. I've found that there are a few simple rules to live by," he said. "Honesty is the best policy, don't eat yellow snow, and finders keepers."

Max smacked Bozeman's hand away from his chin. "Except you didn't find the bag. You stole it!"

"Yes, well, honesty may be the best policy, but dishonesty comes in a very close second." Bozeman bent over and picked up the bag, then shook it out.

"But it's no good to you," said Max. "There's only one person who can work it, and that's Santa."

"Santa? Really? What I understand is that there is only one person who can work it," said Bozeman, "and that person is you. And once you show me how, there will be two of us."

"Even if I knew how it worked, I would never show you," said Max.

"Is that right?" said Bozeman. "You know, sometimes it helps to look at things from—shall we say—a different perspective."

He turned to Dutch and gave him a nod and a wink, and Dutch smiled and nodded back slowly. "Got it," he said.

CHAPTER 29

TAKING THE PLUNGE

Six stories below Bozeman's office stood Baxter, Leoni, and the elves, their necks craned upward, their eyes focused on the rooftop, where they hoped to see Max any second now, riding toward them on Blitzen's back, the red bag safely in his hands. What they saw instead was Dutch holding tightly to Max's ankles, dangling their friend out the sixth-floor window, headfirst, a hundred feet in the air.

"Oh no," Leoni gasped. "They're going to drop him."

"Like a watermelon," Eldor added.

"Please! Don't!" they could hear Max shouting. "I'll tell you everything. I'll tell you how the bag works!"

A moment later, they watched Dutch drag Max back

inside and then slam the window shut.

"Did you hear that?" shouted Baxter. "He's going to tell Bozeman how the bag works."

"I don't think so," said Leoni. "For one thing he has no idea how the bag works. And as soon as Bozeman figures that out, who knows what he might do to Max next."

"We should call the cops," Baxter offered.

"Are you crazy?" said Eldor. "They'll take that bag in as evidence. They'll throw it in a room full of DNA samples and brass knuckles. We'll never see it again. There's got to be another way."

"Wait a minute," said Skhiff, looking suddenly inspired by the sight of a chunk of brick lying near a dumpster a few feet away. He picked up the brick and got a feel for the weight of it. "I've got an idea."

"You're gonna throw a brick at him?" said Baxter.

"Not quite. You guys wait here," said Skhiff. "I'll be right back."

Without further explanation, Skhiff scurried across the street toward a small hardware store.

"Any idea?" said Leoni to Eldor.

"None whatsoever."

Then they watched as Skhiff raised his arm and hurled the brick through the hardware store window.

The burglar alarm sounded, and Baxter, Leoni, and

Eldor became suddenly very nervous about whatever Skhiff might be up to.

"What's going on?" Baxter wondered. "What's he doing in there? He's going to get us all thrown in jail."

And then, in a second, there was Skhiff, climbing carefully through the broken storefront window. In each hand, he held a toilet plunger. "Here," he said breathlessly as he ran up to the parked car and handed a plunger to Eldor, who regarded it with a look of utter confusion.

"We're going in through the toilet?"

"Being small is no excuse for thinking small," said Skhiff. "Follow me."

The elves hurried across the street to the sidewalk in front of Rainforest. Skhiff looked up to the sixth floor. It was windows, large panes of glass, all the way up. And he knew well that there are few things that suction cups like more than smooth, hard glass.

"Okay," he said. "Looks like each floor is about the height of your average chimney. Six floors, so five breaths and we're there."

"So we're not going in through the toilet?"

Skhiff ignored his friend and spit into the plunger.

"Oh, I get it now," said Eldor, spitting into his plunger as well.

"Ready?" said Skhiff. "Upshoot!"

They each inhaled dramatically, and a brief second later, they both shot upward, quickly at first, then slowing as they neared the second-floor windows. They reached out and thrust their plungers at the windowpane, and when they were sure the seal was firm they breathed out. As the helium left their lungs, they became heavier until they caught their breath and were able to inhale again.

"Okay," said Skhiff. "One down, four to go."

They took in another breath, then yanked the plungers from the window and floated to the third-floor window. They repeated the procedure to get to the fourth floor. Now there were just two more to go before they'd be bursting through Bozeman's office window with fists of fury. Flying cartwheels. Enter the dragon.

All was going exactly according to Skhiff's wonderful plan until they yanked their plungers from the fourth-floor window. It was only when they were drifting up to the fifth floor and ready to plant their plungers once again that Skhiff realized the suction cup of his plunger had remained stuck to the last window and what he was now holding, ninety feet above the ground, amounted to nothing more than a useless stick.

When he gasped in surprise, the helium left his lungs and he instantly began to fall. Quickly, he reached out and grabbed hold of Eldor's leg just as his friend planted his plunger on the window.

"What are you doing?" demanded Eldor, looking down at Skhiff dangling helplessly. "You're pulling down my pants."

"I lost my plunger," Skhiff called up.

From across the street, Baxter and Leoni watched with dismay. "I've been thinking," said Baxter.

"About what?" asked Leoni.

"With elves like this, how does Santa do it every year?"

"I don't know." Leoni shrugged. "Outsourcing?"

CHAPTER 30

THE DOWNSIDE OF UPSHOOTING

Back on the sixth floor, Bozeman was rubbing his palms together enthusiastically. "Okay," he said, tossing the bag to Max, who was still hyperventilating from his most recent near-death experience. "Class is in session. I think you'll find I'm a very fast learner."

Slowly, but not so slowly that Bozeman could sense he was stalling for time, Max took the bag by the bottom seam. "Well," he said. "It's quite simple, actually. You see, uh . . ."

"Yes, yes," said Bozeman, leaning closer.

"All you have to do is take the bag like this." Raising the bag above his head, Max began to spin, slowly at first, gradually picking up speed. "And swing it around like this.

You know, to get the energy flowing."

"Yeah, yeah," said Dutch. "I can really feel the energy. This is exciting."

"Okay," said Max, spinning faster with every second. "All together now, say *Merry Christmas!*"

Dutch and Bozeman barely got out the first syllable when toys of metal, wood, and hard plastic came flying from the bag in all directions, bouncing off walls and sending Dutch and Bozeman diving to the floor for cover. Max tucked the bag under his arm and burst into a sprint for the door, stepping hard on the small of Bozeman's back on his way out. But before he could get two feet out into the hall, he hit something resembling a brick wall with legs. It was Lanny, who reached down, grabbed Max by the collar, and with one hand lifted him to eye level. "Going somewhere?" he asked.

"Let me go!" Max protested.

Lanny ignored the order and dragged Max back into the office to see Bozeman and Dutch climbing to their feet, the floor littered with toys. "Hey, looks like you figured out how to work the bag. That's great."

"Shut up!" snapped Bozeman. "Where's the gasoline?"

"It's Christmas Eve," Lanny replied. "Gas station's closed."

Bozeman's face grew redder yet, and he turned and barked at Dutch. "I want you to bring the car around. We're taking a ride out to the dump. The gas station might be closed, but I believe the incinerator is running twenty-four hours a day. We need to make sure that this awful bag is properly destroyed."

"Incinerator?" Max gasped. "You can't do that. You can't destroy the bag. It's the only way Santa can get toys to everyone in the world. You'll ruin Christmas for millions of kids."

"You mean millions of freeloaders," said Bozeman. "Now they can buy their toys like everybody else—from me." He then turned to Lanny. "Keep an eye on this one till we get back."

"Sure thing, boss," said Lanny.

Max watched helplessly as Bozeman, the red bag clenched within his greedy fist, hurried out into the hall with Dutch on his heels.

Just as the inner workings of the bag were a mystery, the exact amount of weight that a plunger stuck to a fifth-floor office window can hold is also currently unknown to science. What is known is that the amount is less than the weight of one scrawny and one overfed elf. With a sharp pop, Eldor's plunger came loose from the window, and for a moment he and Skhiff hung in midair, the small amount of helium in their lungs keeping them briefly afloat.

"If you don't mind," said Eldor, "I'm going to start screaming now."

The two elves began to plummet toward the street below. Luckily they had the good fortune of being completely out of sync with one another, so while Eldor was screaming, Skhiff was inhaling. When Skhiff let out a scream, Eldor was inhaling. This gave them just enough helium to slow their fall as Bozeman's black sedan screamed out of the underground parking garage and headed toward where they were about to land.

Skhiff screamed, but Eldor gasped—that is, he took in one last quick breath—which had the effect of slowing their fall just enough that the speeding car passed directly under them. With a painful *thud*, the elves landed on the car's trunk. Thinking quickly, Eldor planted his plunger firmly on the car's back window. He grabbed on tightly to the plunger handle, and Skhiff hugged Eldor's leg. The car took a sharp left, disappearing from Baxter's and Leoni's sight.

"We've got to follow them," said Leoni, climbing aboard her bike.

Baxter sighed as he threw his leg over his bike. "Who knew that saving Christmas would involve so much exercise."

At that very moment, back in Bozeman's office, Max was getting plenty of exercise himself as he paced nervously about, taking his frustration out on the toys that still littered the floor. He kicked a hard plastic doll, and it bounced harmlessly off Bozeman's desk.

"Hey, easy there," said Lanny, casually leaning back against the door, the only means of escape. "What kind of person kicks a baby?"

"What kind of person ruins Christmas for the entire world?" Max shot back. "Without that bag, Santa can't deliver toys." He glanced up at the hole in the heating duct. If only he were an elf, he could upshoot his way out of there.

"I hate to be the one to break it to you, kid," said Lanny, who had spent his entire life on the naughty list and, as such, never received a gift from Santa. "But there's no such thing as Santie Claus, elves, or flying reindeer."

"Flying reindeer," said Max, the words leaving his mouth involuntarily. "That's it."

Max put his forefinger and middle finger into his mouth then pressed them against his bottom molars and blew. Though the result seemed to be nothing but silence, several neighborhood dogs began barking.

"You shouldn't bite your nails," said Lanny. "Very bad habit."

"Not high enough," Max said to himself. He tried again, and this time the result was absolutely nothing. No dogs barking. Nothing. Zero.

Until a moment later, when the room exploded in a shower of shattered glass.

Max and Lanny dropped to the floor, covering their faces with their arms. When the last bit of pebble-size glass had bounced musically off Bozeman's desk and onto the floor, Max shouted, "Blitzen!" as Lanny slowly uncovered his eyes and realized that there was a real live reindeer standing in the middle of Bozeman's office.

Max sprang to his feet and hurried toward the reindeer, the bits of glass crunching beneath his feet. He brushed a few pieces from his hair. "You did it!"

"Hey, hey. What's going on here?" Lanny demanded.

"Don't worry," said Max as he climbed onto Blitzen's back. "It's like you said, there's no such thing as flying reindeer."

Then Lanny, powerless to intervene, watched as Blitzen, with the boy known as Toy Man sitting on his back, flew out the sixth-floor window.

CHAPTER 31

PLAY BALL

Despite pedaling as fast as they could, and regardless of the fact that they knew all the back alleys and other shortcuts, there was no way that Baxter and Leoni were going to catch up to Bozeman's car. Luckily, they wouldn't have to.

"Hey, guys," is all Max had time to say as he buzzed overhead and around the corner.

"Yay, Toy Man!" Baxter shouted to the sky, pumping his fist.

"Go get him!" yelled Leoni.

Dutch cranked the wheel to the left and took another sharp corner, when something in the sideview mirror caught his eye.

"Hey, boss," he said to Bozeman, who sat in the passenger seat with the bag on his lap. "I'm not sure, but I think we've picked up a tail."

"What kind of tail? Cops?"

"Reindeer."

"What?" Bozeman swiveled around to see for himself and was treated to the sight of two small men clinging to the back of the car by way of a plunger stuck to the taillight.

"What is it?" Dutch asked in response to Mr. Bozeman's high-pitched scream.

"Little men. With pointy ears. On the car," he shrieked. "Get rid of them!"

Dutch swerved violently to the right, then to the left, causing the elves to swing across the trunk, back and forth, screaming all the while.

The car skidded around another corner, and Bozeman screamed again when, inches from the passenger window, he spied Max riding a flying reindeer.

"Hey, Bozeman," Max yelled loudly enough that it could be heard through the glass. "I almost forgot to give you your Christmas present. It's a little early, but you've been such a good boy this year. I hope you like Ping-Pong."

Like a bag of microwaveable popcorn, the bag began to expand in fits and starts until Ping-Pong balls were pouring out by the thousands, quickly filling up the car's interior.

"I can't see!" said Dutch as the level of Ping-Pong balls rose to his chin. Bozeman felt desperately along the armrest for the window button. He found it and quickly lowered the window, causing hundreds of balls to pour out onto the street.

But it was too little too late. The out-of-control car hit a median, causing it to go into a spin. Once, twice, three times around, before it collided with a construction site porta-potty, knocking the plastic outhouse over with an audible slosh.

No one was happier when the car finally lurched to a stop than the two dizzy and terrified elves who had been riding it like a rodeo cowboy aboard an angry bull.

As they slid down from the trunk of the car, its doors flew open and, in a shower of Ping-Pong balls, Dutch and Bozeman crawled out on their hands and knees. Despite all that had happened, Bozeman still clenched the bag in his white knuckles.

But the moment Bozeman stood up, Blitzen, with Max steering him expertly, swept down and, with his antlers, expertly snatched the bag from Bozeman's hands.

Bozeman's face turned redder than it had ever been. He raised his fist to the sky, and just before he could unleash a string of every inappropriate word he was tackled to the ground. Eldor hit him low and Skhiff hit him even lower, and down he went.

By the time Max circled back around and landed next to the car, Dutch was already two blocks away, sprinting as fast as he could down the street, while Eldor and Skhiff were using a spool of bright-red Christmas wrapping ribbon to tie Bozeman's hands and feet.

"Get off me, you little freaks!" Bozeman yelled just before a Ping-Pong ball rolled into his loud, open mouth.

"Good job, guys," said Max. He climbed down off the reindeer's back as Baxter and Leoni rode up on their bikes.

"You did it!" Leoni exclaimed. "You got the bag back!"

"You saved Christmas!" said Baxter, putting his arm around Max's shoulder and pulling him closer.

Besides Bozeman, there were two others not sharing in the joy of the moment. Skhiff pushed his sleeve back and checked his watch. "Don't get too excited," he said. "We still gotta get the bag all the way back to the Pole, and it's T-minus twenty minutes."

"Oh no," said Eldor. "When the old man notices the bag is gone, he's gonna roast our chestnuts over an open fire."

CHAPTER 32

SECRETS REVEALED

Just as Eldor and Skhiff had finished securing Bozeman's hands, it began to snow. Not a little but a lot. Whereas most snowstorms start out gradually and build in intensity, this one seemed to arrive all at once. And with it arrived the sound of bells, lots of them, like a hundred tambourines growing closer and closer until, finally, in the distance, Max and the others could make out the outline of something very familiar.

It was a large red sleigh hitched to seven flying reindeer. And driving that sleigh was me, your trusty narrator. Max, Baxter, and Leoni watched, unable to speak, as my sleigh circled once around, then made a perfectly silent landing next to Bozeman's car.

"Hey, boss," said Eldor with a tense chuckle. "We were just talking about you."

"Yes, I heard that," I replied. "And, for the record, you're right. Your chestnuts are so roasted." I climbed down from the sleigh and regarded the three starstruck children standing before me. "Hello, Max," I said. "Leoni. Baxter."

Baxter responded with an audible gulp. "You . . . you know our names?"

"I know a lot of things," I explained. "I know when you're sleeping, I know when you're awake, I know when you've been bad or good, yada yada yada."

"Right," said Max. "Then you must also know that I didn't steal your bag. I found it."

"Well, that's not exactly true," I told him. My response seemed to hit Max like a punch to the gut.

"It is true," Max insisted, tears filling his eyes and spilling over. "I swear it. I found the bag."

"He totally did," Leoni said. "Me and Baxter were there when it happened."

I noticed Max's knees trembling as I stepped toward him and placed a hand on his shoulder.

"You didn't find the bag, Max," I repeated, softly this time. "The bag found you."

"But I . . . what?"

"As our wealthy friend Mr. Bozeman is fond of saying,

there are a few simple rules to life," I said. "Honesty is the best policy, don't eat yellow snow, and finders keepers. The bag found you, Max. Just like it found me, a hundred and twenty years ago."

The look of sadness left Max's face in exchange for one of confusion. "I'm sorry," Max replied. "I don't understand."

"I think what he's saying is," offered Eldor, "that we didn't lose the bag, the bag lost us."

"No, you lost the bag," I said sharply. "And don't ever do it again."

Eldor and Skhiff looked nervously at their shoes as I held out my hand to Max, who happily relinquished possession of the red bag. "You see, Max," I continued as I inspected the bag for damage. "I'm actually Santa Claus the sixth."

"The sixth?" said Leoni. "You mean . . . there's more than one of you?"

"Well, only one at a time," I clarified. "But even we Santas eventually retire. And when we do, the bag seeks out and finds a suitable replacement."

Max brought his hand to his chest. "So, you mean I'm . . ."

"Santa Claus the seventh," I answered, carefully folding the bag, satisfied that it was free of damage and otherwise completely intact. "Think about it. Didn't you wonder why you were the only one who could work this thing? Or why you were able to ride Blitzen? Or why you knew what all those kids wanted without having to ask? It's because you, Max Fernsby, have been chosen."

"Chosen?" said Max with the exact amount of skepticism appropriate for such a claim.

"Yeah, I have to admit it sounds pretty crazy," I said. "And all I can say is that the bag has never once made a mistake, and I have no reason to believe it has this time. After all, you've got everything it takes. You're smart and self-sufficient, with a strong desire to travel the world and the ability to put the needs of others ahead of your own. Not many kids would have done what you did."

As the words left my lips, I realized that I'd almost forgotten. I held up my right index finger as if to say, "Wait a minute, I'll be right back," then turned and walked to the sleigh. I reached inside and scooped up the puppy, whose tail had been wagging ferociously at the sound of Max's voice.

"Plato?" Max gasped at the sight of him. He breathed so deeply that it looked as though his chest might explode.

"You gave up your dog for the good of the world," I said, reuniting Max with his puppy, who greeted him with excited whimpers and slobbery licks to the face. "And let me tell you something," I added, "it's not easy driving a sleigh with only seven reindeer while a dog is chewing on the seat."

"But how did you . . . ?"

"There are a lot of things we Santas can do. And eventually you'll learn them all. That is, if you want the job. You'll have to relocate to the North Pole, of course. But your friends are welcome to visit anytime they want."

"Well then of course he wants the job," Baxter blurted.

Of course, Baxter's opinion wasn't the important one. It was Max who would have to be convinced.

"Well?" I said. "What do you think, Max?"

"All the parts of the universe are moving," Max replied. "All you have to do is jump on and go for a ride."

"Should I take that as a yes?"

"You should definitely take that as a yes."

Baxter and Leoni squealed with glee and executed a perfect high five. "One question," said Baxter once the dancing and hugging had come to an end. "Can we still call him Toy Man?"

I looked at Max's chubby friend and shrugged. "Sure thing, Bag Boy. As for you knuckleheads—," I said, turning my attention to the two elves.

"We know, we know," said Eldor. "Off to Greenland with us."

"Greenland?" I scoffed. "You two have held just about every job there is at the North Pole. As a result, you know more about how things work than almost anybody. That's why I'm putting you in charge of training."

"Wait a minute," said Eldor, not sure if he had heard me correctly. "Are you saying that we're gonna be training the new Santa Claus?"

"That's right," I confirmed. "And if you screw it up, I will personally kick your lime-green butts all the way to the South Pole. Is that understood?"

"You can count on us," said Skhiff. The two thoroughly relieved elves snapped to attention and delivered a sharp salute.

"Good," I said. "Because thanks to you I'm already two hours behind schedule. "Now don't just stand there. Get Blitzen harnessed up so Max and I can be on our way."

"You mean, I'm going with you?" asked Max. "Tonight?"

"It is Christmas Eve, isn't it?"

"It sure is," said Max, brushing off the snow that had accumulated on Plato's curly head.

I walked back to the sleigh and climbed into the driver's seat, then leaned over and offered Max a hand.

"All you have to do is jump on and go for a ride," I said.

Max took my hand and stepped aboard, tentatively at first, as if he were still not a hundred percent sure that any of this was actually happening.

"Listen you two," I called out to the elves, who were just finishing their task by placing the bit into Blitzen's mouth.

"Make sure our friends Baxter and Leoni get home safely."

"Sure," said Skhiff. "But how do *we* get home?"

"We'll pick you up on the way back," I said.

"Okay," said Eldor. "But what about him?" He gestured toward Bozeman, who was writhing on the ground, his cursing interrupted by the Ping-Pong balls that rolled into his mouth each time he opened it.

"He looks like a hard worker," I said. "I'm sure we can find something constructive for him to do. Now try to stay out of trouble till we get back."

"Aye-aye, sir," said Eldor, stepping away from the sleigh.

"Hey, Max," Leoni called out. "Good luck. And don't forget, I've been very good this year."

"No," said Max with a smile. "You've been great. Both you guys."

"Hey, leave us something special," said Baxter. "So we know it was you."

"Sure," said Max. "Okay, guys. I'll see you soon. Merry Christmas."

"Merry Christmas," said Baxter and Leoni together as my sleigh sped off down the street, then slowly lifted into the air and vanished from their view into the swirling snow.

CHAPTER 33

ANOTHER FIRST

The early morning Christmas Day sun reflected off the snowy rooftops of Paris and cast the Eiffel Tower in a golden glow. If people passing by had bothered to look up, they might have seen the sun's rays reflecting off the glass in the frame of the small photograph. Tied with wrapping ribbon to the very top of the steel structure, it was the picture of Max and his mother; the one taken in New York with the Statue of Liberty in the background as the two smiled broadly, never happier.

Meanwhile, halfway around the world, Baxter was smiling too as he ran through his apartment on the way to the mantel, where his stocking hung above the gas fireplace.

He had never before seen his stocking quite so stuffed.

Sticking up among all the presents, some wrapped and some not, was a postcard. Baxter plucked it from the stocking and looked at it carefully, which is when he realized it wasn't really a postcard but a photograph. It was a selfie Max and I had taken together, each of us offering a smile and a thumbs-up with Machu Picchu right behind us.

"He was here! He was here!" Baxter shouted loud enough to jolt his sleepy mother from her bed.

On the back of the picture, Max had written his friend a message. "Peru was awesome," Baxter read. "And Paris was beautiful. Saw some whales near Australia. Hope you like the special present. Your pal, Max." Baxter lowered the picture, then thought a minute. "Wait. Special present?"

With a closer look at his stocking, Baxter noticed that, ever so slightly, it was moving.

By the time Baxter could get himself sufficiently bundled up to finally go outside, he found Leoni already running down the street toward his apartment building.

"He was here!" she shouted.

"I know," Baxter replied. "Check it out."

Leoni gasped when Baxter removed his right hand from his coat pocket and there, clinging to his thumb, was a tiny squirrel monkey.

"He brought you a monkey?"

"He brought me a monkey!" Baxter exclaimed while performing an elaborate victory dance. "How about you? What did he bring you?"

"Come on," Leoni said, her eyes sparkling with excitement. "I'll show you."

Baxter gently placed the monkey back into his pocket, then took off after Leoni as she ran to the end of the block and around the corner. "Wait up!" he called out, but Leoni was too excited to slow down. By the time Baxter finally caught up to her she was standing in front of the fort. "What? What is it?" he panted.

Short of breath herself, Leoni simply pointed to the spot on the chain-link fence where the For Sale sign had hung. The sign now declared the property sold. Next to that sign hung another, which read, "Future Home of the Leoni Malone Civic Youth Center."

"Wow," said Baxter. "That's pretty epic all right."

"Yeah," Leoni agreed. "Now finally there'll be something for kids to do in this neighborhood."

"Seriously, is this just the best Christmas ever?" Baxter gushed.

"Yeah," said Leoni, with less enthusiasm than Baxter expected. "I guess so. But it is missing one thing."

Baxter slowly nodded. "Max," he said.

"I wonder what he's doing right now," said Leoni, looking in the direction she imagined was north.

"What do you think he's doing?" said Baxter. "He's at the North Pole, hard at work, training to be the next Santa Claus."

Baxter was perfectly right about one thing. Max was at the North Pole, under the strict tutelage of Eldor and Skhiff, who, at that very moment, were sprinting across the frozen ground. On their faces was a combined look of abject fear and intense joy.

"Whoo!" cried Eldor. "Run faster, Max!"

Max did as his teacher instructed and picked up the pace as Plato ran beside him, yapping happily.

"Another first!" Eldor cheered.

"You'd better hope we don't get caught," Skhiff huffed and puffed as the village came into view. "They'll put us back on poop duty."

"No way, junior," said Eldor. "I believe that position has already been filled."

As they scampered past the stables, there he was, holding a shovel in his white-knuckled hands, his face as red as a pomegranate.

"This is unacceptable," said Bozeman. "Don't you know who I am?"

A grizzled old elf named Trov took his eyes off the spectacle before him just long enough to poke his head through the stable door.

"I know who you are," Trov said. "You're the guy who needs to shut up and start shoveling reindeer poop. Those poinsettias need fertilizer now."

"Well, if you'd stop feeding these four-legged freaks so much, maybe I could keep up," said Bozeman. Through clenched teeth, he turned and snarled at Dasher like a wolverine, which he instantly realized was a mistake. The reindeer responded with a sharp kick that sent Bozeman blasting through the stable wall and into a snowbank.

He looked up weakly in time to see Max and the elves running into the village square, toward the meeting hall, while an angry polar bear in a jeweled tiara and a bright-pink tutu lumbered right behind.

And so there you have it. The heretofore untold story of that magical red bag that, as you now know, transports toys directly from the North Pole and, every hundred years or so, seeks out and finds a worthy successor to aging

Santas like myself. Of course, it'll still require many years of training before Max is able to fully take over and perform this very demanding job on his own. So I'll be staying on for a bit and working side by side with him until he's old enough to get his sleigh license and grow a decent beard.

I'd love to tell you more about all that, but I'm afraid that's a story that will have to wait for another time, because right now I have to run. Literally. As it turns out, there is such a thing as too many Christmas prunes.

Merry Christmas,

Santa Claus VI

ACKNOWLEDGMENTS

The authors would like to give special thanks to the two Davids who made this book possible. To super agent David Dunton, who delivered the manuscript into the very skilled hands of editor extraordinaire David Linker, who helped shape it into the book you now hold in yours.